LIFE'S A
BEACH

Also by Chloe Coles

BOOKSHOP GIRL

LIFE'S A BEACH

CHLOE COLES

A BOOKSHOP GIRL NOVEL

First published in Great Britain in 2018 by
HOT KEY BOOKS
80–81 Wimpole St, London W1G 9RE
www.hotkeybooks.com

A CIP catalogue record for this book is available from the British Library.

ISBN: 9781471407338
also available as an ebook

1

Printed and bound in Great Britain by Clays Ltd, Elcograf S.p.A.

Hot Key Books is an imprint of Bonnier Zaffre Ltd,
part of Bonnier Books UK
www.bonnierbooks.co.uk

Note from Chloe

As any Bookshop Girl will tell you, seeing your own book published and for sale in real-life bookshops is one of the coolest dreams that could possibly come true. (Even cooler than waking up one day to find that you live in an edible house made of Kinder Buenos or something.) And what's even cooler than THAT, is the fact that I'm here writing an introduction to ANOTHER book. Another story featuring best friends Paige and Holly as they temporarily break free from their bore-off hometown and set up shop at the seaside.

I love the seaside. Like, I really, really love it. Maybe it's because I grew up in Northampton, which is 'landlocked' and a full on TREK away from sticks of rock and penny pushers and those ridiculously delicious hot greasy donuts you get in paper bags on the pier.

I love the seaside as much as I love charity shops and chips and boys in Harrington jackets and reading (of course) and I've stuffed all of these favourite things into the pages of this book.

I hope you like it. And if you don't and you've binned your receipt, well it's probably too late for that anyway.

Chloe x

LET'S GO, GIRLS

'Crap! I totally forgot to pack sun cream!' My best friend Holly panics through a mouthful of Cool Original Doritos, sunglasses sliding down her nose.

I squint at the gloomy clouds through the window of the train and wave goodbye to stinky old Greysworth, which is shrinking further and further into the distance.

'Holly. Look around. It's October. I don't think you'll need your factor fifty.'

'It's not a real holiday without the *smell* of sunblock though, is it?!'

'Well . . . we could just pretend that we're on some chic city break. And that we've packed trunks filled with vintage fur coats and Dr Zhivago hats . . .' I glaze over, imagining that the rows of patio gardens and abandoned trampolines whizzing by are actually snow-covered pine trees.

I mean, really, it's not like we're about to catch a plane to some wild bender in Magaluf or set sail on a once-in-a-lifetime, all-expenses-paid trip around the Caribbean, like the ones you can win on daytime telly competitions.

Nope.

It's way cooler than that.

Me and Holly have blagged ourselves half term at the Skegton-On-Sea Book Festival!

It's one of the biggest book festivals in the country; authors and journalists and TV presenters flock from all over to be there. Tickets *always* sell out within the first hour of going on sale because the festival has such high-profile guests.

I found that out the hard way, staring in disbelief as the SOLD OUT message flashed on my phone screen in the middle of a French lesson.

'*Ça va, Paige?*' Monique, the class *assistante*, asked as she knelt beside the bubble-gum encrusted desk, watching me groan in despair. I mean, it was all *her* fault. If she hadn't picked on me to join her in some cringey role play *à la pharmacie*, then I'd have snagged tickets for me and Holly before it was too late, rather than wasted precious moments of my life making up a French word for Strepsils. (Turns out it's just *strepsiles*, by the way.)

We had been so prepared. The events programme had been announced weeks ahead of tickets going on sale and as soon as we heard that our all-time favourite (and most dreamy) hot shot author-illustrator, Johnny Hoxton, was flying in to do a talk and promote his brand new book, we knew we had to be there – front and centre.

Tickets for the whole week cost one hundred pounds. That's right, one *hundred* pounds. One hundred and *one pound fifty* if you count the booking fee. Think of the millions of Freddo Frogs and penny sweets you could blow that on.

We both work part-time at Bennett's Bookshop, and signed up for all the extra hours we could get just so we had enough money for those tickets. We unpacked crates of heavy new books before college. We vacuumed the shop after the last dawdlers had left the building and we even missed Gracie Partridge's rainy birthday BBQ just so that we earned double pay on the bank holiday weekend. But all for nothing.

After we lost out on tickets, we were gutted for approximately an hour and a half, until lunch break that same day. But as we slumped on blue wheelie chairs in the common room, I had an idea.

'We *will* get there, Holly.'

'How do you mean?' She gasped as she burned the roof of her mouth on a baked-bean panini (one of our school canteen's delicacies).

'Think about it: we are Bookshop Girls! Books are what we *do*! If we can't get into the festival as fans, then we'll get in there as *booksellers*. As industry *insiders*.'

She nodded, eyes wide and cheeks stuffed like a hamster, before swallowing a hot lump of cheesy beans dramatically. 'Maybe Tony knows somebody at the festival who could sort us out . . .'

It turned out that our grumpy bookshop boss *did* know the woman who coordinates SBF (as those in the know call it). They 'went way back' according to Tony, who shifted uncomfortably and adjusted his glasses as we begged him to put our names forward. He *ummed* and *ahhed* at first. Warned us that it's a lot of hard work. Really full on. It's not like Greysworth. He said he wasn't sure it was a good idea, seeing as both of us are still under eighteen. There might not be someone on hand to supervise us. He didn't know if we'd cope.

I reminded him that we're beyond capable and very mature for our age *and* that I was told by my orthodontist that I only have to wear my retainer three nights a week, which technically makes me a WOMAN, and he squirmed and said he'd see what he could do and the rest is history.

We'll be manning a bookstall, selling the relevant novels to festival bookworms and setting up stock to be signed by big-shot writers. It's basically like we're being PAID to go on a BFF HOL and SELL A FEW BOOKS! GET IN!

We've never actually been on holiday together before. Well, not if you don't count the residential trip to Milton Keynes Outdoor Adventure Centre in Year Six. That was different. We didn't really *want* to spend a week building rafts while teachers wore jeans and hoodies, masquerading as Normal Human Beings. What's so great about building a *raft* anyway? This will be way better. Our first holiday. Just the two of us. Not a sick bucket in sight.

'I wonder what our festival boss will be like . . .' Holly opens another bag of train sweets.

'Tony didn't give much away. Let's just hope she loves spontaneous karaoke without the actual backing tracks and celeb spotting as much as we do.'

'Oh, I have something for you to add to The List,' my partner in crime announces, making grabby movements with her fingers for me to pass her my sketchbook.

I pop the clasp on my new-old suitcase.

I bought it in a charity shop especially for this holiday. It's a vintage powder blue hat box with a rubber handle. I cleaned the outside of it with a face wipe. The inside is made of fabric so there wasn't much I could do there but spritz a bit of perfume around and hope it didn't make my clothes smell like the manky old cuddly toys in Save the Children.

My sketchbook is squashed inside the case. It's not a coursework book for school. It's a moleskine one. A5 size. Dog eared. And it's filled with scribbles and notes. It's got a few bits of life drawing from the Posers class we go to, but mostly, really, it's a bit like a diary, but with more pictures than words. I draw customers from Bennett's. I draw wiggly outlines of what I imagine fictional characters from books to look like. It's got clippings from magazines and newspapers and quotes that I like and there are things like sketches of my brother, Elliot, when he'd fallen asleep in front of the telly.

It's the closest thing I have to a diary. I tried writing diaries when I was younger but would lose interest after a couple of days. It's safe to say there wasn't much going on in my life besides winning the occasional raffle in assembly. (The prize was a bumper pack of multi-coloured Sharpies, so I'm not knocking that at all.) If I was still in Year Six this sketchbook would have a little padlock on it to keep it secret. I don't really show it to anyone. Only Holly is allowed to see inside and, well, that's mainly because she just brazenly walked into my bedroom, opened it up and helped herself to my private thoughts. It's too late to keep anything from her now.

The List is scrawled inside. Holly's tongue juts out in concentration as she adds to The List with a Bennett's Bookshop Biro.

Find out if Tony and our festival boss were romantically involved.

Ew. My best friend is such a creep sometimes. One of the many reasons we're inseparable.

The rest of The List is things we want to see/eat/ Instagram while we're on this holiday. It is constantly edited and expanded. What started off as a fun to-do has turned into this huge epic saga.

Here's a few things we've included so far:

<u>Get as many selfies with famous people in the background as poss.</u>
Target: At LEAST 20.

<u>Win the jackpot on the 2p machines.</u>

Self-explanatory really. It's a seaside town. Surely there will be amusements. Surely *somebody* has to win on those penny pushers. Right?

<u>Sample chips from every chippie in town.</u>

Rate them out of ten. We are chip connoisseurs. We KNOW the best chippie in Greysworth is Billy's Fish Bar on the market square. Now that we're exploring a new town, and a seaside town at that, we must find the finest chips. Judged on saltiness, sogginess, tastiness. We'll find the best in Skegton.

<u>Learn to love mushy peas.</u>

This is Holly's entry and she refuses to remove it from the list despite the fact that I've told her NO ten thousand times. No way. I'm not on board with that. Way too green and way too gross.

<u>Smash the patriarchy.</u>

This is just on my daily to-do list so it should go without saying but it feels good to tick something you know you'll do anyway. Like *get up* or *brush teeth*. Zero tolerance for crusty male privilege? Tick.

We take it in turns to play *Guess What Song I'm Lip Syncing To* and Holly wins because I can't resist doing Britney every time and as everybody knows it's scientifically impossible to do Britney without the head movements. She fist-clenches along to some mystery power ballad as I pull her headphones out.

'We are now approaching Skegton-On-Sea. Doors will open on the left-hand side. Please ensure you collect all of your belongings before leaving the train.'

'We're here!' I jump out of my seat and we frantically shove the evidence of our chocolate feast into the little flappy bin.

We stretch our legs on the platform and take it all in. It feels like we've just walked onto the set of *The Railway Children*. It's so quaint and old-fashioned. The only clue that we're not actually about to run along the tracks with Bobby, Phyllis and Peter is the big orange vending machine and the discarded McDonald's paper bag that glides along in the breeze.

'Breathe! Breathe it in!' Holly inhales dramatically. 'That seaside air!'

I copy her. I close my eyes and let the cold wind batter my cheeks. Picture myself as a Disney mermaid, all scales and shell-boobs, washed up on a big rock and doing the best hair flick of all time.

'Right. Yes. Yeah. Thirty crates should be arriving later today. We need access to the cafe tent . . .' A woman speaks into a phone and walks straight towards us.

Holly looks at me for an explanation and I shrug.

Still fully involved with the convo on her phone, this woman stops before us, flashes a smile and holds out her hand, as if for me to shake.

'Right, okay, thank you. Do not be late.' She ends the call and grabs my hand. 'I'm Penny. Head of Ops at Skegton Book Fest. I take it you're Paige and Holly from Bennett's Bookshop in Greysworth?'

She talks without breathing and it throws me. I stumble over my words. 'Yes. Oh hi. Yes, I'm Paige.'

'And I'm Holly. Thanks for having us.'

'Not at all. Thanks for helping out.'

This is when I notice that she has one of those earpiece thingies in her ear. It's attached to a microphone that clips around her neck, like she's performing at the Brit Awards or something.

'There is so much to do. Follow me, this way, I'll show you to your accommodation.'

So *she's* our festival boss.

'She doesn't strike me as someone who'll be up for karaoke with us, Hol,' I whisper.

'Well, that hands-free mic begs to differ! It's official: I'm making it my mission to have a go on that thing before we're back at this station.'

I snort and double step to keep up, lugging my hat box after me.

SEA VIEW LODGE

The festival is happening in the grounds of this really grand hotel called . . . The Grand Hotel. We checked it out on Google. It looks out onto the seafront and has big fancy gardens with coiffed hedges and stone statues of women with ice-cream-scoop boobs. It's the kind of place a girl on *Don't Tell the Bride* would dream of tying the knot, despite the fact that her groom will inevitably plan to do the deed underwater in some grotty leisure-centre pool.

We won't be staying there. The budget didn't stretch that far, so our accommodation is apparently just a black pudding's throw from where we'll be working.

While Penny marches at least ten paces ahead of us and sighs, explaining that 'We neeeeeeed at least twice the number of chairs,' to some poor idiot on the phone, we anticipate what the Sea View Lodge holds in store for us.

'Maybe it'll be some hip minimalist Airbnb with Scandinavian furniture and a host called Claus . . .' I suggest.

'Yes! He'll wear a jumper slung over his shoulders and drink tiny espressos!'

As dark clouds loom above, we get our first real glimpse of Skegton-On-Sea. We pass a couple of decent-looking charity shops, a chippie that smells like HEAVEN and about twelve different tattoo and piercing studios.

Holly squeezes my arm and even though she's still wearing sunglasses I know that her eyes are bulging with excitement. '*Matching tattoos!*' she hisses.

I laugh it off, already dreading the thought of needles and appearing on some future late-night TV show about inky regrets.

'Look, Hol! It's the sea! *The sea!*' I squeal. Icy, choppy evidence that we're miles away from crappy old Greysworth.

'The sea.' Holly takes a deep breath. 'Watery home to old nappies, empty cans of Fanta . . . and the necklace from *Titanic* . . .' She sighs. 'Ain't she a beaut!'

Penny has her call on speaker phone and holds it to her mouth. She makes demands in very clipped sentences.

'Deliveries at the back. Three pallets by two thirty AT THE VERY LATEST. All trestle tables out of storage asap.' She looks like those contestants on *The Apprentice* who never hold a phone to their ear like normal people. I tried it once – the speakerphone, limp wrist, casual chat thing. Backfired. My mum asked if my tummy was feeling better or if things were still 'explosive' at the precise moment that a group of sixth-formers joined me in the bus shelter.

As Holly and I take our billionth selfie of the day – this one different to all the others because SEA – I hear Penny wrap up her phone call.

'This is it, girls. Here we are.'

Penny's hair is short and grey. It picks up in the sea breeze and stands on end. She frown-smiles. Y'know a frown-smile; it's the kind that you usually only see from PE teachers or dinner ladies. I silently pray that Penny doesn't prove to be as sadistic as one of those pole-vaulting, cauliflower-cheese-vending monsters. She leads us up a gravel path towards Sea View Lodge.

Not a Claus or a tiny coffee in sight.

It smells like air fresheners and has clashing floral wallpaper and carpets. I'm going to Instagram the *mothballs* out of this place.

Holly and I are sharing a twin room. Chintzy, floral bedspreads and a vase of artificial flowers. There's an en-suite and a wall-mounted telly. The height of sophistication. We've got a mini bar containing one tepid can of Pepsi. Oh, and a tiny mirror with a handy plug for straighteners and a pine desk with Sea View Lodge stationery in the top drawer.

Our room is at the back of the building. A twitch of the net curtain gives fantastic views of the car park tarmac. There are only a few cars out there now but Penny warns us that the place will be rammed tomorrow when the festival kicks off.

'I'll give you girls some time to freshen up and get changed into these.' She hands over a couple of bright red T-shirts that say BOOK FESTIVAL STAFF on the back. 'Meet you by the box office in about half an hour?'

Her phone rings and she waves goodbye to us before picking up with a 'Yes?'

As soon as Penny closes the door behind her, Holly kicks off her sandals (yes, really, sandals in winter because HOLIDAY) and leaps onto her bed.

'We're not *actually* going to jump up and down on the beds like this is a bad road-trip movie from the noughties, are we?' I question, slipping out of my shoes, all too ready to pounce.

'We *have* to jump up and down on the beds or it's bad luck!' Holly sings as she scrambles on top of the nylon bedspread.

TOTEBAG OF DOOM

We Google Map our way to the festival. It's only a short walk but I spend most of it hoping that one of the huge seagulls ahead doesn't swoop down and peck me to death. The bright red book-fest T-shirt means I could be easily mistaken for a bag of Walker's ready-salted crisps. I pull my leopard-print coat tighter around my chest to protect myself.

'Oh my God, look at this place!' Holly grins.

We find the cluster of marquees and tents that have popped up in the grounds of the hotel. Blokes in polo shirts and cargo trousers with pencils behind their ears load cables and tables and bits of stage out of white vans. Penny explains that as the festival opens today we'll be getting to work straightaway as she gives us a quick tour of the place, always a few paces ahead so we have to practically run to keep up with her. There are three different venues within the grounds. One is a thing called a Spiegeltent. It's all shiny and old fashioned, with wood panels and mirrors and stained glass. Folded chairs have been set out in a semi-circle. Penny tells us that there's going to be a spoken-word performance taking place in there later and Holly's face lights up. (She's been writing her own poems since she got all loved up with Official Boyfriend, Jamie. She puts on this weird voice to recite them. Doesn't really sound like her. It's funny. And hugely impressive, I'm not gonna lie.) Then there's the Main Stage tent. When we stick our heads around the door to this place I'm amazed: it's like Doctor Who's Tardis or a Narnian wardrobe or something. From the outside it just kind of looks like a circus tent without all the fun stripes, but inside it's massive.

'It feels like a proper theatre.' Holly smiles. 'Like the one at home.'

She's talking about the Albany in Greysworth, the place we've spent every Christmas of our lives watching X Factor rejects do panto.

'C'mon, girls, there's more to see this way . . .' Penny tears us away from the stage and shows us the cafe tent. They have muffins and salted caramel brownies and posh crisps and baristas wearing black trousers that definitely double up as school uniform during term time. Holly gives me a not-so-subtle nudge as we pass a couple of lads stocking bottles of organic apple juice into the big fridges. Two nudge-worthy boys in less than two hours of being here. That already beats the sixteen-year average of Greysworth sightings.

Not that I'm *bothered*.

It's clear to me that romance is just a big fat waste of time. Like shaving your legs in winter or sitting non-calculator Maths exams. Useless. Pointless.

What I learnt from art-school wannabe Blaine Henderson – or He-who-shall-not-be-named (which is what I'd refer to him as, if I actually wasted precious breath on speaking about him) – is that I really nearly fudged up EVERYTHING by getting sucked into his swirling vortex of dreaminess. It almost cost us the whole campaign to save Bennett's from closing, and he just turned out to be a massive let-down.

I can't let that happen again. So I'm steering well clear of romance.

It's kind of hard to block it out when Holly and Jamie have been an actual Facebook-official BF and GF couple for three months now. They post selfies with cute snapchat filters that make them look like loved-up squirrels. They had a day trip to London and walked around Covent Garden holding hands. I swear, I did not hear the end of how Holly's bag got jammed in the underground train doors as they closed and Jamie managed to prise them open and saved the day because he's such a hero and his arms are so strong since he's started working part-time as a lifeguard at the Kingsthorpe Leisure Centre.

Aside from those two, sticking to my romance-free rule isn't *that* hard in Greysworth. It has an extremely low population of Boys To Fancy, which means that I don't have a queue of hunky lads lining up to save me from being dragged along a train track in the Big Smoke.

I avert my eyes from the apple-juice boys and perv on the lemon and poppy seed muffins instead. Safer. More reliable. Who needs lads when you can have cake?

'Now *this*,' Penny waves her clipboard towards a building that looks a bit like a big greenhouse, 'this will be your home for the next few days.'

There's a blue neon sign above the double doors. THE BOOKSHOP TENT.

It's way bigger than I expected it to be. The ground is bumpy and uneven, but that's just because it's carpet rolled over soggy grass. The shelves are already set up but our job for the day is to unpack all of the books and put them on display.

I think we're going to *love* it here.

'Girls, these are for you.' Penny hands us festival programmes.

We thank her and open them up as if it's the first time we've seen them. As if we *didn't* spend a lunchtime in the sixth-form common room printing them out then highlighting the events we wanted to make in order of preference.

'And this bag contains all you'll need for the rest of the week.'

It's humungous. So heavy it just about pulls my puny arm out of its socket. A canvas totebag filled with Book Fest Essentials.

'The cashbox is in here. I need one or both of you to bring this back to the box office every night once we close the shop, okay?'

There are card machines and rolls of receipt paper and spare Biros and Sharpies for signings and this old-fashioned carbon paper in case one of those card machines doesn't work because apparently the signal can be dodgy in this area.

I hope Holly remembers all of the important stuff

Penny is telling us, because even though I'm trying my hardest to pay close attention, I'm buzzing. I'm way too excited to actually be here. It's like we're being left to run our very own bookshop. Just me and Holly. It's a dream come true! I've always wanted my own shop. When I was younger, my favourite game was 'shops'. I'd force my little brother to be my one and only customer, and he'd have to pretend to pay for my Beanie Babies or Sylvanians with those big plastic coins. He'd get pretty restless and ask if he could put his toys in my shop and buy them. I'd say no, because it was My Shop and I didn't sell Playmobil.

Obviously, this is much cooler. Not only do we practically have our own shop, but, like, it's at one of the coolest, biggest book festivals in the country. With actual literary legends. SO much more exciting than what we're used to, and hey, even THAT can be pretty cool as it turns out.

Breathe, Paige. Calm down.

'Now, I'll be around if you need me. If there's anything at all you're not sure about, please let me know. I'll have my walkie-talkie on me at all times, and yours is in there, just as I've explained.'

What? We actually have walkie-talkies? And she's already explained that to us? Wow, I really haven't been paying attention at all.

Penny's phone rings and she dashes towards the door, only answering with a, 'YES, I'M LISTENING.'

Holly turns to me and we squeal. We're here!

I gasp. Literally gasp when I see it.

'Holly, LOOK!'

I'm on my knees, delving into a crate of Johnny Hoxton's *Rock'n'Roll Sketchbook*! This is the book we've been waiting for and it's here, in my hands, four whole days – that's ninety-six hours – ahead of official publication date!

Johnny Hoxton is a legend. He's famous for being in an iconic indie band – all long, floppy hair and pouts. They split up a few years ago and this is his first ever book. I suppose that makes him a celebrity author. The kind of guy that my colleague at Bennett's, Adam, would roll his eyes at as if to say, 'Typical.' Whatevs, Adam, it's not like the manic-pixie, big fringe and glasses girls he crushes on are anything out of the ordinary. And the thing is, Johnny Hoxton is an amazing artist. I wish I could draw like him. I flick through the pages of his work. I want to know what kind of ink he uses.

'Oh, Paige. It's beautiful.' Holly kneels beside me and takes a copy of the book, turning it over in her hands like it's a lump of solid gold.

'This has made my day.' I clutch the hardback to my

chest, barely able to open it, the anticipation is too much.

'This is what we came for!' She mock-cries happy tears. Come again – maybe she's not faking it. Her eyes are wet. 'I could die a happy woman right in this moment, Paige Turner.'

'Um, HELLO? I think you're forgetting something pretty maje, Holly.' I blink in disbelief. 'He's going to be *in here*, in this very tent, breathing the same air as us, so please make sure you survive until then.'

The cover of Johnny's book is a life-sized portrait of his face. So gorgeous. Holly holds it up in front of her face so that it looks like she's Johnny Hoxton from the neck up, and that she's, well, Holly from the neck down.

'Paige Turner,' she puts on a gravelly voice from behind the book, 'it's such a pleasure to meet you at last . . .'

'Oh, J-Ho,' I play along, 'please believe me when I say, the pleasure's all mine!'

Holly makes muffled air-kissy sounds from behind the blurb and I blow kisses her way when all of a sudden:

'*Oh, hellooooo!*'

Our obsessive fan-girling is interrupted by somebody entering the tent, carrying a trestle table.

Caught in the act, Holly jumps to her feet and throws the book to the ground. I shudder and hold my copy close to my bosom. I always knew I was the more loyal fan between the two of us.

'I'm Tim,' the stranger continues, puffing out his cheeks under the strain of the table until we try to help him, and shuffle it into position. 'You must be the Greysworth girls! Well, it's nice to meet you.'

He shakes my hand and I always try so hard to make sure I have a good strong handshake. It probably doesn't even matter in real life what your handshake is like unless you're a contestant on *Dragons' Den* or something, but I'm a self-conscious shaker. So I squeeze a bit as I do it.

As Holly introduces herself, I have a look at Tim. He's tall and bounces on his knees as he walks. He's a grown man, probably in his forties. He has hair the colour of wet sand, tied into a long ponytail that falls between his shoulder blades, which jut out in his red festival T-shirt. He tells us this is his twelfth Skegton Festival, and that he works in the local bookshop in town with Penny.

He hums a tune to fill the brief silence and taps the trestle top with his long, sinewy fingers. 'Well, this'll be your desk, and I'll bring you another one in for the signings.'

'Will the signings be in here?' I ask, way too excited at the prospect of actual famous authors being in the same room as me.

'Ooooh yes!' says Tim, raising his eyebrows. 'We use the Main Stage tent for some of the very big names, but most authors are happy to work in here after an event.'

As he leaves the room, Holly holds the Johnny Hoxton book in front of her face, so that it looks like his face is her face again. 'Just think,' I hear the muffled excitement from her hidden face, 'I will be RIGHT HERE, SIGNING!'

BOOK FEST REALNESS

Day One of Book Festival Life and well, it's harder work than I thought it would be.

For a start, no one told me there'd be *Maths* involved. That's enough for me to back right out of any situation. Enough for me to pack my belongings into a hanky on a stick and whistle as I trot off into the sunset.

It's never been my strong point. And in the festival bookshop there's no computer to tell me how much change I need to give. We only have this ancient metal cash box and have to work it out for ourselves.

Prior to this, I have only ever used the calculator on my phone to split the bill at Wagamama's. Now I'm tapping furiously on the screen every time somebody approaches the desk with a stack of freshly signed books, all selling for various prices.

I get this prickly feeling of dread every time a customer tells me they have the extra ten pence *if that helps*. It never helps. I only just scraped that Maths GCSE and every time I fumble over twenty-pence pieces in the cash box, I can see Mr Evans' snarky know-all face, the kind that only a Maths teacher can have, saying, '*See, you do need Maths in everyday life.*'

Luckily Holly's here to help, just like she was when we started big school, and I needed her to actually count the coins out of my denim Hello Kitty purse to pay for a jacket potato in the school canteen.

The two of us decide to take a quick, much needed break while the shop tent is quiet for the first time all afternoon. Everybody seems to have filed inside the Main Stage tent to watch a panel of writers talk about frontline journalism, whatever that is. I put my feet up on a spare chair, delving my arm inside a can of Sour Cream & Chive Pringles, which initially I always hate. They're a gross flavour and they stink like old knickers but once you pop you can't stop and you actually can't taste or smell anything any more either, so here I am, gobbling them up like there's no tomorrow.

Like there's no tomorrow and no Ross Kemp lookalike about to burst into the room, soaking wet from the downpour . . .

'Hello!' Holly stands, dusting her salty hands on her black tights. 'Can I help?'

'Hello, ladies.' The wet, bald man shuffles his shoes on the door mat. He's wearing a black suit and has a wire poking out of his collar and into his ear. 'I'm Lady Rockwell's bodyguard, Reggie.'

REGGIE?!

A BODYGUARD?!

LADY ROCKWELL?!

Before I can even mouth, *But who the hell is Lady Rockwell?* Holly nods and beams.

'Great,' she says, like she actually knows what he's talking about or something.

'Shall I bring her this way?' he asks, chewing gum as he talks. 'She's in the car outside and is keen to have a look around before her first event tomorrow afternoon.'

'Sure.' Holly smiles.

As soon as Reggie dashes out of the tent and towards the mysterious car, Holly shuffles through event programmes and paperbacks, searching for clues. *'Which one is Lady Rockwell?!'* she hisses.

'I have no idea! I thought you knew!' I panic, wiggling my arm out of the Pringles tube.

The name doesn't ring a bell.

'Here she is!' Holly unfolds the festival brochure and points to a page titled *Fifty Years of Bodice Ripping* with Lady Minnie Rockwell.

Okay, so she's a romance novelist.

'LOL! Wonder why Penny booked her.' I chuckle. 'Maybe Tony's not the only one who gets her hot under the collar!'

I jump out of my Pringle-dust-coated skin when I see her. She looks mad.

She's old. I don't mean teacher-old, I mean *old*-old. Like she-must-be-in-her-nineties-old. That's not what makes her look mad. I can feel my mum tutting at me for that even being a suggestion. That's not what I'm saying. It's what she's wearing that makes her look so . . . nutty.

She moves towards the bookshop tent tentatively, shuffling a bit like ET when he's in baby Drew Barrymore's clothes. Her bodyguard holds a pink umbrella above her head, while his own bald scalp is splattered with huge, heavy raindrops.

Her entire ensemble is pink. Pink pink pink.

Pink like Barbie pink.

Before I know it she's inside our book tent and is carrying this little dog around in her pink, manicured claws. It's blond. I've never thought of an animal being blond or brunette or anything as human as this one. It's so well groomed that it puts the entire cast of *Love Island* to shame.

Dame or *Lady* or *Queen* or whatever kind of Rockwell she is, she is large, but not tall. She makes our bookshop tent feel minute all of a sudden. Her perfume fills the air – and it's the proper stuff, rather than the celebrity fragrance they push on you at the Superdrug counter. She smells expensive.

A pink pill box hat with pink flowers sits still on top of her peroxide-dyed mass of grandma curls. Pale, glittery blue eye-shadow all the way up to her thin, drawn-on eyebrows. Black eyeliner. Thin fuchsia lips. Her rubbery neck is dripping in pearls and diamonds that look so shiny I can't tell if they're actual real posh ones or the kind I used to cut out of the Argos catalogue to make mood boards for my home-made Barbie outfits. To be honest, she does look a bit like something eight-year-old Paige would have dreamt up.

Holly and I watch. Take it all in. Gulp, and swallow our crisps hard. She's like nothing I've ever seen before.

LOVE'S SWEET ARROW

I can't rely on Holly to do the talking this time – she's clearly as stunned as I am.

I clear my throat, but before I can say 'Welcome to Skegton' or curtsey or kiss her feet, Penny swings into the tent, attaching her radio to the waistband of her black jeans.

'Lady Rockwell, what a pleasure it is to meet you. I'm Penny – I coordinate the Skegton Book Festival.'

They shake hands.

'Hello, dear. This is my secretary, Geraldine.'

I hadn't even noticed the other woman. I've been blinded by Lady Rockwell.

Geraldine nods and smiles with her lips pursed. She wears her silver hair in a bun tied at the nape of her neck, and a cream cashmere two piece with a grey knee-length skirt. Her rectangular glasses sit perfectly on the bridge of her nose and the creases in her natural-look tights fold into McVitie's Digestive wrinkles above sensible shoes. She must be older than my gran but she's still a few centuries younger than Minnie. Compared to her boss, she looks as fresh faced as a pre-mugshot Justin Bieber.

This wasn't something that we'd paid any attention to when I printed off a copy of the events programme at school and Holly went to town on highlighting the talks we wanted to see (colour coordinated in order of importance – pink for things we would rather die than miss, then yellow for second priority, then orange). The fact that the festival was celebrating some sort of anniversary of Minnie Rockwell's career was something we overlooked. I mean, it's not like the entire book festival is dedicated to her or anything, there are hundreds of interesting people appearing over the next week – hundreds of people we highlighted in florescent pink. But as Minnie points her spindly finger at two bald delivery men struggling to carry a pink marble desk towards a tent that is purely for Minnie fans to gather in, it's easy to forget that I'm not lost at Minnie Fest.

'It's quite the sight, isn't it?' Tim chuckles, hands on his hips as he watches the commotion in the rain outside.

Minnie's dog barks and the marble-table men slide in the damp, muddy grass.

Fifty Years of Bodice Ripping with Minnie Rockwell. According to my well-thumbed festival programme, the talk isn't until the end of the week, but there are signings and readings leading up to this. Despite the fact that she's been going at it for half a century, she's not about to give up – Minnie has an action-packed schedule for the week, starting with a writing workshop this afternoon. Penny has asked if I'd watch the bookstall at the back of the marquee while the class is on, which will be an opportunity to *add strings to your cupid's bow, with the guidance of romance literature's best-selling author.* Groan. Obviously I'd rather be working in the bookshop tent with Holly, on the lookout for Johnny Hoxton to appear, but I'm way too intimidated by Penny to say no.

Slumped in my plastic chair with period pains from hell, feeling like I have one of those push-along lawnmowers tearing up my insides, I watch Minnie Rockwell guiding a tent full of fans through what it is that makes her this fluffy pink ball of success.

'I do believe, that one of the most important elements of conjuring love stories, is to have your body relaxed . . .'

She's reclining on a chaise longue. I've never been to a writing workshop before but I'm pretty sure this isn't the usual setup.

'This is how I write my stories, you see. I lie on my back like this and I close my eyes . . .' Her watery irises disappear behind wrinkly eyelids, thick with shimmery shadow. '. . . I close my eyes and I dream of wild, romantic love affairs. I don't ever pen my ideas – it's far too much of a distraction – I dictate them to Geraldine and she types it all up.'

Geraldine nods solemnly.

How mental is that? Minnie just lies around all day and comes up with a load of hearts-and-flowers crap? The audience are gobbling it up and actually taking notes, like this is something they can all try themselves! If I suddenly started lying around on the carpet, cooing on about 'love's sweet arrow' and 'raging loins' my mum would actually fire me as her daughter.

A lady in the audience raises her hand to ask a question. She's got a tissue stuffed into the sleeve of her cardigan. 'Hello, Miss Rockwell. Firstly I'd just like to say that I'm a huge fan of your work . . .'

Minnie nods, used to the admiration.

'Well, you've written so many exquisite novels over the years . . .'

'One hundred and twenty-nine, darling,' Pink Lady Rockwell confirms.

'What advice would you give to other people who want to pursue a career in romance fiction?'

Minnie flicks her powdery blond curls and sings, 'Listen, my dear, you're never too old to *feel*. I'M SEVENTY-SIX AND AREN'T I WONDERFUL!' It's not a question. It's a statement.

I don't think I've ever come across someone as full of themselves as she is.

This is so lame. As if I've been lumbered with some loved-up romance author when Holly gets to stay in the bookshop tent eating muffins from the hot cafe boys. NOT that I'm paying any attention to the hot cafe boys.

After the questions, quiet descends in the writing workshop. The audience sit at their folding trestle tables, writing their own saucy tales, following Minnie's instructions. The only sound is the rain outside, and that snotty little dog pawing away at Lady Rockwell's large, bejewelled bosom.

I open my sketchbook to a crisp blank page and write my own piece.

MINNIE ROCKWELL: THIS IS ALL ONE SWEET, HOT, THROBBING LOAD OF RUBBISH.

Once the session is over, and I've sold TWO books (waste of time, turns out most of the fans have their own well-loved copies already), a woman with shiny brown hair and red lipstick approaches Minnie gingerly.

'Lady Rockwell?' she nearly whispers. 'Hi, my name's Amanda Jackson.' She holds out her hand to shake and Minnie looks her up and down through those thick, tarantula lashes. 'I work for *Glambag* magazine and was wondering whether you'd allow me to interview you for a piece on your legacy as a feminist icon?'

Minnie rolls her eyes at this and sighs. 'Amanda, darling, I wouldn't rule it out completely, but you'll have to talk to my secretary, Geraldine.' She waves her wrinkly hands, shooing the journalist away like she's some irritating fly. 'Geraldine!' she howls, despite the fact that Geraldine is literally right behind her. 'Geraldine! Take this lady's details.'

A feminist icon.

I pick a book from the stack of Minnie Rockwell novels. The cover illustration is some nineteen-seventies-style painting of a woman dressed in a big frilly skirt, bosom heaving over the top of her corset, hair in ringlets around her face, running her fingers over the bronzed, bare chest of some big long-haired hunk.

Glancing around to check if anyone's watching me dip into erotic fiction with a cover as cringey as this, I think, *Well, maybe it would be interesting to see what all the hype's about . . .*

LiTTLE STiCK OF SKEGTON ROCK

My back is kuh-illing me!

'How did I get saddled with the Totebag of Doom?!'

'Give it here, I'll have a go. We should take it in turns.' Holly hulks the killer tote of bookshop tent essentials onto her arm and I rotate the shoulder I've permanently damaged by carrying it this far.

Embarrassingly, my massively impractical Primark slip-on shoes make this kind of farty, squelchy noise as Holly and I trudge over the muddy tarpaulin floor away from the marquees.

'It's my shoes,' I clarify. Just in case she thought we'd reached a new level of our BFF-dom where I was comfortable enough to freely let rip in public.

She yawns. 'Today was intense.'

Yes, it was. In a matter of hours, we unpacked and

shelved even more books onto the display units. We made a long list of what titles need to be where and when. We piled up tons of Signed Edition stickers and we unfolded chairs and we even created a huge pyramid of hardback fantasy books big enough to make those really massive airport-sized Toblerones look puny. We even smirked our way through random passages of Minnie Rockwell's romance novels. It was all duchesses and heaving bosoms from what we could see.

Palms up to the sky, I fill my lungs with that salty sea air. 'As much as I do genuinely want to gorge on a luxurious Domino's delivery and watch our way through the vintage VHS collection back in our hotel room, now that the rain's eased off, maybe we should *explore* . . .'

'Take me to the sea!' Holly sings, linking her arm in mine.

Holly's family always go on holidays to Spain. They'd *always* go during term time when we were younger. Holly said her mum said it's cheaper to do it then. *My* mum said it was irresponsible to take your kids out of school and that it was Bad Parenting. I obviously didn't tell Holly that. I didn't care that it was Bad Parenting. I *only* cared that it made a week feel like an eternity. Counting down the PE lessons I had to suffer without my partner in crime until she came back to school with a tan, those holiday braids in her hair and a transfer tattoo of a dolphin or a star, carefully unwashed and preserved for me to marvel at. One time she brought me back a trinket box covered in tiny seashells. I still have it. I keep all sorts of treasures in it – an old Polly Pocket, spare tampons, hair grips and lipsticks in shades I don't have the lady-balls to wear during daylight. It's so cool to be on holiday together.

Skegton-On-Sea isn't much, but it's everything we want it to be: it's anywhere but Greysworth.

Along the high street, we tap on the windows of charity shops that have closed for the night, eyeing up second-hand tea sets and LOL-bad CDs we remember from primary school. We stumble around the amusement arcades, giddy from our flutters on the 2p-coin pushers. (I just frittered away three quid in a pointless attempt to win the fifty-pound note that was hanging over the edge.)

When we emerge, it's raining again.

Big, heavy drops of rain splatter on the tarmac promenade in front of us.

Heavier and heavier.

We need somewhere to shelter before the rain gets the better of our fringes.

I dash towards a place with a candy-striped awning. The front of the shop is clad with soggy postcards, plastic sandcastle buckets in netty bags and Skegton-On-Sea magnets.

I pull Holly inside, out of the downpour.

The door pings as I shake my umbrella and Holly twists her hair into a bun.

Wow.

This place is rammed floor to ceiling with STUFF. Souvenirs and toys and beach accessories. Keyrings and shelly picture frames and those bottles filled with colourful sand.

We have stepped into a glistening palace of tat.

An old lady sits behind the counter, sipping a cup of tea. She looks up from her crossword and nods at us. 'Hello.'

We nod, mouths agape with astonishment. We are Dorothy and Toto, outside is black and white Kansas, and this place . . . this is Oz. Technicolor munchkins and yellow bricks and joy. We've been swallowed into this belly of Skegton-On-Sea memorabilia.

I spin countless wire racks of postcards to find the ugliest, tackiest one to send to my brother. Bingo. It's a cartoon of a jellyfish wearing a bikini. *Fish You Were Here* . . . Sold. I'll write, *LOL, Elliot, didn't know you'd been to Skegton-On-Sea before! This is a well nice photo of you. X.*

I wander through the maze of T-shirts and postcards and armbands and cuddly toys and –

'Ooooh! Oooh! Look at these!' Holly pulls me towards a wall of multi-coloured rock. She waves a shiny pink stick of cellophane-wrapped candy and shows me. 'It has my name on it!'

I take a closer look. So it does. Through the middle, tiny, perfectly formed red letters spell out HOLLY.

How do they do that?

'Let's find a Paige one!'

We scour the plastic baskets until we find a yellow stick of PAIGE rock and I jump up and down with joy.

'Okay, we're not leaving until we find a personalised stick of rock for everyone back at Bennett's in Greysworth.'

With our bags and coats and phones sprawled across the shop floor, we navigate our way through the A-Z of handwritten signs (as booksellers, alphabetising is Our Thing so we should be good at this, right?) and collect sugary pressies for all of our Bennett's family.

We find an ADAM and a BRIDGET and even a BRUCE. We can't find a TONY stick of rock so we settle on SWEETHEART for him instead. I cannot wait to see the expression on his face when he sees that. I imagine it'll be somewhere between his usual bewilderment and disgust.

We pose for selfies in Skegton-On-Sea baseball caps. We shake Skegton snow globes frantically.

Holly smirks as she points to a corner of merch labelled ADULTS ONLY. There's a bountiful wealth of rude sweets and lollies. Before I can say *Bubblegum Breasts*, Holly is wiggling a penis-shaped marshmallow lolly in my ear.

She puts on a posh voice, Minnie-Rockwell style. 'The count wiggled his throbbing member at the duchess!'

We are helpless with laughter. I have tears rolling down my cheeks.

I barely even notice the twitch of a beaded curtain behind the old lady at the till.

I barely notice the boy who emerges.

Barely.

And then all too quickly I am very aware of the boy behind the counter.

'Nan, your programme's on now . . .' he says.

His eyes are on me and Holly.

I stand, mouth open, with a penis-shaped lolly poking me in the ear.

OH MY COD

'All right then, love. You can take it from here. Don't forget to chain up the postcards outside.' The old lady wraps her cardigan across her chest and shuffles through the beaded curtain towards the hum of a soap theme tune.

I may be the grand old age of sixteen (and mostly retainer-free) but I still feel that BUZZ of excitement/danger/mischief when there are no adults around. It's just us in here. Me, Holly and that total BABE of a boy behind the till. Oh, and the marshmallow dick my best friend has failed to remove from my ear.

I snatch it out of her hand and chuck it back onto the display. It's the kind of thing you wish could be done so quickly that no one notices, but all the cellophane packaging made it very squeaky and he's defo seen us fannying around in the ADULTS ONLY section.

Because he's sat behind the counter, I can only see the top half of him. With roughly fifty per cent of boy in my vision, I'm one hundred per cent certain that he's really gorgeous. He's got shortish, floppy brown hair. He's wearing a checked shirt, buttoned all the way up to the top, a small Fred Perry emblem embroidered on the left side of his chest.

He smiles. You know that kind of half-smile that boys do? Just one side of their mouth twitches upwards. Blink and you miss it. I reflect it right back at him, but there's a reason I don't usually do the half-smile – it comes out a lot twitchier than anticipated.

'Hi.' Now he's actually smiling.

'Hey.' And I'm grinning.

Be cool, Paige. Who needs lads when you have cake, right? Remember that?

Shame I don't have any lemon poppy seed muffins on me right now.

I watch as Holly unloads the armfuls of tat we've decided to spend our hard-earned cash on out onto the counter. Yes, she is actually buying a Skegton-On-Sea fridge magnet.

'What? I'm starting a collection.' She blinks at me, seeing my surprise.

'Since when?'

'I have a Gran Canaria magnet from my nan. Now I have this. Two makes it a collection.'

The boy at the till doesn't say much as he prices up our souvenirs and puts them into a candy-striped paper bag. We are buying A LOT of rock. I think he's smirking, though. Yep, he's laughing at the SWEETHEART rock, and the one that Holly picked out for Jamie. It's red and says HOT STUFF on it. Jesus. It is pretty embarrassing. Not that Holly seems to notice. She's living in HOT STUFF-SWEETHEART world though, isn't she? Which is exactly where I don't want to be, which is exactly why I'm not checking out this lad one little bit, nope, not for me.

It's taking him ages to tap the prices into the till.

I feel like I want to say something – to let him know that FYI those aren't sweets for my boyfriend. That I don't have a boyfriend, as it happens. That I'm single . . .

'That's seven pounds, please.' He's got an incredibly drool-worthy northern accent.

I remember that we're splitting the cost. My purse is in here somewhere. It's always right at the bottom. I take everything out of my bag, handing things to Holly and balancing objects one by one on top of the counter as I shove my arm further down into the depths of the Totebag of Doom.

'Johnny Hoxton,' the boy says, looking at the book I've placed precariously on the surface.

'Um, yeah.' I blink. 'It's his new book.'

'We're working at the book festival in town,' Holly explains with a cool confidence, since she's used to hanging around with boys now because of Jamie. The fact she's talking gives me a bit of a kick up the bum to join in instead of just standing here gawping.

'Are you a fan?' I attempt to ask but my throat is suddenly really dry and it comes out more like the croak of a toad than an actual human sentence.

'What?' He looks at me with these sparkly Slush-Puppy blue eyes. It's hypnotic. Like the tanks of rotating ice they have in the corner shop across the road from school.

I clear my throat. 'Do you like Johnny Hoxton?' I ask the boy at the till.

'Oh, yeah, I mean, his band were decent . . .' He says 'decent' like it actually means GOOD. Nobody would say that in Greysworth. How exotic. 'I didn't know he was an artist too . . .' He shrugs.

'I'm starving.' Holly moans, clutching at her belly.

'So where's the best place to get chips around here?' It feels pretty glam to ask a local where to get something 'around here'.

Skegton boy scribbles a map on a paper bag, and it's at this very moment that Holly mentions she's 'partial to a battered sausage'.

I stamp on her foot and she howls. Christ! I thought she was the one who knew what to do in moments of Hot Boy Proximity.

We have to get out of here before she blurts any more OBSCENITIES in the presence of this lad. I rush us out of the shop and into the rain.

Despite how kind it was of Souvenir Shop Fittie to draw out directions for us, Holly and I still get lost. Twice. (It's fair to say that he's no Johnny Hoxton when it comes to drawing.) We eventually find ourselves outside a chippie called Oh My Cod. Oh boy, does it smell like heaven.

There's a cartoon fish painted on the glass door, its little fin smacked against its mouth. Can fish feel OMG-able? Do you think they ever experience cringe-worthy mortification? They probably would be mortified, actually, if they found out they were about to be nestled up with a load of yummy potato and gobbled up by two hungry girls.

'I think we're going to like it here, Holly.'

We huddle over beige polystyrene boxes of the soggiest,

saltiest, tastiest chips. Holly zigzags ketchup all over them like a maniac, but honestly, I think they're so delicious and fresh that you could eat them naked. We bob up and down to stay warm and dry, working the tiny wooden forks from our fingerless gloves.

Skegton boy might be crap at directions, but he has excellent taste in takeaways.

THE DEFAMATION OF PEPPa Pig

OMG. When I open my eyes the next morning, it takes me a second to remember where I am.

Not in my usual bed in my room at home, nope.

I can hear seagulls and snoring. Holly's snoring. I turn over to catch a glimpse of her in her bed, rub my smudgy eyes (my mum would kill me for not taking my make-up off last night) and check the time on my phone.

WTF!

We slept in! We were supposed to meet Penny at the bookshop tent TEN MINUTES AGO.

I leap into action, yelling for Holly to wake up.

We pull our manes into heaps on top of our heads, roll deodorant over unwashed pits and share the sink to brush our teeth. Just a flick of Rimmel London eyeliner and no one would know that it took us seven whole minutes to get our bums into gear.

I can't believe we slept through our alarms. It must be that sea air. We may also be slightly concussed following our attempts on the dodgems last night. Brutal. Remind me to never drive a real car. I'm wincing every time I move my neck, like one of the people in those TV adverts asking, '*Have you been injured in an accident at work that wasn't your fault?*'

We're nearly ready to roll. Holly fannys around with the DO NOT DISTURB sign on the door handle, when I wonder, 'Where's the Totebag of Doom?'

'What are you on about? I thought you had it.' She points at me.

'Crap! No, I don't!'

We thrash around the room, turning it upside down – pillows, socks and hairbrushes flying.

'Holly!' I stop searching for a minute to laugh as she flings a pair of wellies out of her suitcase and onto the patterned carpet. 'WELLIES, THOUGH?!'

She shrugs at me.

'No way.' I shake my head in disbelief. 'As if you had room for those as well!' I mean, I know I packed light in order to fit a whole wardrobe into a vintage hat box because AESTHETICS buuuut . . .

'Excuse me, Paige, I think you'll find that wellies are a festival-chic STAPLE . . .'

'It's a *book* festival. In a tent. Pretty much indoors. It's hardly the Pyramid Stage at Glasto.'

She grimaces. 'I think we must have left the Totebag of Doom in town somewhere last night.'

I try not to hyperventilate – that old goody-two-shoes part of me rearing its You're-going-to-get-into-soooo-much-trouble head.

We're too late to do anything about it now, and can only dash through the carpeted hallway past the smell of warm buttery croissants and bacon without stopping.

'I could murder a chonion slice from Gregg's right now . . .' I groan as my stomach churns with hunger.

'You can take the girl out of Greysworth . . . but you can't take Greysworth out of the girl!' Holly chuckles.

I narrow my eyes into a scowl. I've spent my whole LIFE wanting to get out of the tragic hellhole that is Greysworth . . . but then again, she does kind of have a point. I've also spent my entire life in a town that often feels like it has more branches of Gregg's than actual living people.

When we reach the main office, Penny rushes over, shaking her head at her iPad. 'Girls, thank God you're here at last! This is an absolute nightmare! We've got fifty odd kids turning up in the next half hour expecting to meet Peppa Pig and our actor, Paul, has just called in sick. Winter vomiting virus.'

'You mean Peppa isn't *real*?!' Holly mocks as she makes up for lost time, stuffing festival programmes into free totebags.

'You mean Peppa is actually a man called Paul?!' I laugh, but Penny doesn't.

'Girls.' She turns to us, lips pursed. The desperation in her eyes lets me know exactly what she's thinking.

'Please, don't look at me!' I squirm, the thought of slipping into that costume already making me itch uncomfortably.

'We *need* a replacement pig. Desperately.'

'Nope!' I hunch my shoulders, try to hide behind the stack of books on the trestle table so she can't see me but she can totally still see me.

'I would actually just get in there myself if I didn't have to chair the New Voices panel in the Spiegeltent. And I know that Tim *would* be up for it but he's too tall to fit inside . . .'

'Pink just isn't really my colour . . .' Holly shrugs and looks at me.

Nope. No way. No, I'm not doing it. No.

I know that *technically* we should both be jumping at the opportunity to butter up Penny. After all, we *did* misplace the Totebag of Doom last night, and therefore have no idea where the cash box is right now . . . and if it really is gone forever, then we can sing a big Von Trapp '*So long, farewell, auf-wiedersehn, goodbye*' to ever setting foot inside another branch of Bennett's again. If Tony finds out that we were getting giddy on the dodgems rather than guarding the cash box despite my You-Can-Trust-Us speech, then he will surely kill us. Like, actually murder us and chop us up into little pieces and hide all of those pieces in places no one will ever think to look. Like Bennett's. No one will look for my dead body in Bennett's because once Tony finds out we've lost the bag and the cash I can kiss goodbye to my job. Which is a fate worse than death when you're stuck in a town like Greysworth.

So, we need to do the Peppa thing. But if either of us should do it, it's Holly.

Holly.

She owes me. She owes me for the time I lied to Mrs Fowler and said she hadn't asked for our French homework to be handed in that day, JUST so Holly didn't get in trouble for not doing it, EVEN THOUGH

I'd spent all night getting my head around feminine plural nouns.

She owes me for the school library book she took out ON MY CARD before spilling an entire can of Dr Pepper over it, resulting in my year-long suspension from borrowing and a life-long subscription to death glares from Karen the librarian.

She ALSO owes me ninety pence for that Greggs iced finger I bought her last week. I was willing to let it slide but when push comes to shove . . .

Well, that's the last time I agree to settling something with Rock, Paper, Scissors.

Thanks for ruining my life, *paper*.

This is definitely NOT what I signed up for when I volunteered to work at this festival.

I thought I'd be hobnobbing with famous authors, laughing at intellectual jokes, pretending to actually *like* red wine – NOT sweating my trotters off inside a fictional *pig*!

Holly holds my hand and leads me towards a stage because I can barely see through the meshy eyeholes. It's so hot inside this costume. And it smells a bit like

Pepperami. Maybe that's what Paul, the vomiting Peppa Pig impersonator, smells like. Dear Lord.

I crane my MASSIVE head towards Holly's voice in an attempt to understand what it is that she's saying.

'Just smile and wave.'

I take a few clumsy steps as she pauses.

'Well, nobody can actually tell if you're smiling inside that thing. Which is a bit unnerving TBH.'

Nope. Nobody can tell if I'm smiling or crying inside this monstrosity. That's lucky, because I swear to God I'm close to tears. My eyes are definitely wet, but that could just be sweat. Sweaty eyeballs. First time for everything. This twenty-four-hour anti-perspirant is really being put to the test. I doubt that the developers at Dove considered this sitch when creating the product. You won't catch *this* on any adverts for a deodorant they make out is all sassy and fun.

As Holly reads *Peppa Loves to Read* to the audience, I try to block it out. Could anything actually be worse than 'wiggling your wiggly tail' as fifty screaming toddlers clap with joy at your public humiliation?

Once I saw this documentary about people who had been captured and held in prisoner of war camps. One man said that the only way he managed to survive was by counting to ten in his head over and over. That if he could just get through the next ten seconds, then that was okay. He'd managed it. He would get to ten then start again.

I count to ten about A MILLION TIMES until Holly reaches the end of the story.

Thank *fudge* that's over.

I start to leave but then Holly hisses at me – through my eye hole so I can hear – 'They want more, Paige! We have to give them *more*! I'm sorry, what else can I do?!'

The audience chant and I feel beads of sweat roll down the back of my neck. I'm unable to do anything about it while Holly sings, 'Okay, kids, who wants to hear *Peppa Loves to Read* one more time?'

'MEEEEEEEEEEEEEEEE!!!!!' The kids roar relentlessly and I grimace inside this burning pig-shaped version of hell.

I try to count to ten some more but mostly I'm thinking about what a bad vegetarian I am to silently pray for the slaughter of an innocent animal. I am that animal. I am that pig.

Somebody put me out of my misery, please!

The demonic crowd clap and cheer, and Holly takes my fuzzy pig hand in hers and leads me off stage as I gingerly place one foot in front of the other in escape.

She squeezes my arm as she utters something inaudible.
What?

I could swear it sounded like she said, 'OMG, it's that guy!'

Who?

Oh God, maybe it's our manager Tony. Maybe he's somehow found out that we lost the bag and he's legged it all the way from Greysworth to personally murder me.

Holly's talking to someone now. I can't see anything inside this costume. All I know is that she's using the tone of voice she only uses for her boyfriend, Jamie. All sweet and syrupy like a Starbucks Frappuccino with extra whipped cream and those little bits of chopped-up nuts.

'Ummmm, yes, Paige is here . . .' I can't see who she's talking to but I can just about hear her gritting her teeth.

I focus. There is a boy's voice. Low and croaky. And EXOTIC. 'I think this belongs to you. I found it last night. You left it behind at my nan's shop.'

Oh.

My.

'Thankssomuchyou'realifesaver!' I fumble to pull off my Peppa head and see The Cute Skegton Souvenir Boy right here with the Totebag of Doom in his arms.

My human head pokes out of Peppa's huge shoulders

59

and I'm so hot that I can feel my fringe stick like PVA glue to my sweaty forehead.

Oh. I'm talking but I don't know what I'm saying.

It's so bright without this mask on.

I feel –

It feels –

BLACKOUT.

I open my eyes and I'm on the ground, looking up. There's a swell of concerned faces staring back at me.

'Paige? Paige! Drink this.' Holly passes me a plastic cup of orange juice and I sip it, confused.

I must have fainted.

Oh God.

The realisation sinks in.

I'm still Peppa Pig from the neck down.

I can hear toddlers crying in the distance.

'Are you okay, Paige? Did you hurt yourself when you fell?' Holly cradles my damp head in her arms.

Luckily Peppa's bum is pretty Kardashian size-wise so it cushioned the blow. 'I'm fine.'

'Cute Boy's gone to fetch a festival first-aider.'

Oh no! He would have seen! He would have watched my red sweaty head emerge from a pig costume and then pass out. 'What have I done?' I wince at Holly.

She shrugs. 'Well, you left a room full of toddlers scarred for life and robbed them of their innocence. But on the plus, I'm pretty sure you're excused from work-related public humiliation duties for as long as you live . . . so that's something.'

MODeL ViLLagE

I got some chocolate out of it, which is pretty *decent*,
I suppose. Tim is a trained first-aider, with certificates to
prove it. Once I'd wriggled out of Peppa's humungous
body, he sat me down on a folding chair and gave me a
Mars bar, which was really kind because I think it was
something Tim was planning on eating himself – the
dessert element of his packed lunch. Penny said she was
sorry for asking me to wear the costume and insisted that
I take the afternoon off to rest.

Is it wrong to admit that I'd feel one hundred per cent
crappier and more miserable if I was walking away from
the Skegton Book Fest *without* this total fittie wandering
in the same direction as me?

Hate to admit it. *Loathe* to admit it. But it's kind
of exciting.

We didn't, like, *intend* to walk together. Well, it was never my intention, anyway. I was just sloping off, feeling sorry for myself, when The Fittest Boy in Skegton sort of jogged to catch up with me and said he was on his way back to the shop, which is in the same direction. We're walking side by side now.

'So, you're a Peppa Pig impersonator?' I feel him look at me sideways as we trudge past an out of season ice-cream van and a sign for donkey rides that only happen in the summer.

'That was a one-off!' I snort. 'I'm pretty certain that I'll never have to do it again . . .'

'What's your name, by the way?' he asks me. Just like that.

'Paige. And yours?' I ask. Dead casual. Like I didn't Google 'Cute Boy Names' last night in an attempt to guess his with Holly.

'Robbie.'

Robbie. Robbie. Robbie.

'Cool.'

'You're not from round here?'

'No, we're just here while the festival's on. I'm from Greysworth . . .' I explain.

'Greysworth? I think I've heard of Greysworth before . . .' His voice drifts.

'No you haven't!' I laugh. 'No one has!'

'Well, it cannot possibly be any better than Skegton-On-Sea.' He chuckles sarcastically.

'Did you grow up here?'

'Yes. There's no reason I'd be stuck here by choice.' He winces, hands in his pockets.

'It's not that bad. I mean, both me and my friend are pretty excited to be here. For the books.' I shrug. Playing this down. Playing this whole thing down like I didn't count the weeks, days and hours until we boarded that train here.

I hope he doesn't notice as I smooth my hair with my fingers, all too aware that the pig-costume sweat has dried and caused my fringe to separate in all kinds of ridiculous directions.

'How are you feeling now?'

'Oh, much better thanks.' I smile, though I'm gutted to be leaving Holly behind, heading back to the hotel for a rest while she sets up the signing tables for some historical-fantasy author and a kid's TV presenter who has written a book about football-playing porcupines.

Still, it could be worse. *Robbie* and I walk in silence for a while and then I spot something on the other side of a low, neatly trimmed hedge.

'Oh wow, what is *that*?!'

He laughs. '*That* is the Skegton-On-Sea model village.'

It's a tiny model of a little town, with tiny houses and tiny roads and a tiny amusement arcade.

'No way!'

He pushes the white metal gate and motions for me to walk through first.

'It's amazing . . .' I gush, bending my knees to marvel at the teeny-weeny version of the town we're in right now. 'Who made this?'

'It's old. From way back when. Not a true portrayal of Skeggy these days. Look closely – there's not a Poundland in sight.'

The normal-sized raindrops that have landed on the tiny church roof look monstrous, like they could take out a whole congregation of tiny people.

He points out all of the landmarks to me. A bird's eye tour of the town. He gestures at one last thing.

I push my hair behind my ears to keep it out of my eyes. 'What are we looking at?' I lean closer to him to see.

'Down there, next to that little white building – that's where we're stood right now.'

I laugh along. 'Oh wow! And there are even two little people down there!' We look at the miniature, featureless metal figures. 'Whooooah. How meta! Okay, well that's my mind blown for the day.'

Laughing, he slumps onto a damp bench. I've been warned about cold benches like this. I've heard that they can give you cystitis – hellish burning pee for days. I'm not sure if it's a myth, but right now it's a risk I'm willing to take as I plonk myself next to him.

'Is this what Legoland is like?' I ask.

'Dunno. Never been.'

Silence. We stare out at tiny Skegton. My heart beats in my throat. Is this amount of silence terrible? Should I fill the silence with something?

Ummmm. Say something, Paige.

Cystitis.

Not that. Do not say that.

Best to just keep quiet I reck—

'I used to come here a lot as a kid. It's a bit lame, innit.'

I shake my head. It's not lame. It's the furthest thing from lame.

'It freaked me out, feeling so big, like,' he continues.

'I love it.' I grin. Then explain. 'I feel like I've been living in a model village my whole life. I've always felt too big for it.'

I stare at the mini town, and can feel his eyes watching

me, feel his gaze on the side of my face as I speak. 'But, like, *this* –' I gesture towards the little houses and shops and streets – 'this is perfect, because it makes it look so easy to walk out of that town. It would only take a few giant strides and then I could be anywhere in the world . . .'

I turn to face him, cringing, because that monologue already has me kicking myself, no matter how honest it felt before it came out of my mouth.

'I've never really thought about it that way . . . but I definitely think you could do that,' he says, and I feel like I've been hit by a bus. A really fit bus in a Fred Perry shirt and an earring. 'I want to get out too. That's why I started working in the souvenir shop. To save up for my bike.'

He produces a picture of his pride and joy on his phone.

'It's a sixty-eight Vespa. It's beautiful. Gets me around town but won't get me much further until I get a new engine on it.'

Oh God, he's got a bloody moped. This is too dreamy and too ridiculous. I'm starting to feel faint all over again, and now for entirely non-pig-related reasons.

SPOILER

Robbie slips his phone back into his pocket and we sit in silence again.

He jiggles his right knee up and down with his arms folded and I try my best, my very best, to be a normal person casually sitting on a bench.

'What's this?' Robbie nods towards the book poking out of my bag on the bench.

It's one of Minnie Rockwell's books. I may have wanted to see what all the fuss is about, but I didn't really want anyone to *know* that I was doing that. I mean, talking to people about books is one of my favourite things to do under normal circumstances, but do I really want to talk to *Robbie* about *this one*?

My cheeks prickle. I feel myself turning the same shade of hot pink as the book that is now in his hands. I cringe at the amorous couple on the cover illustration. Their public display of affection suddenly seems even more ridiculous out here in daylight than it already did back in the festival tent with Holly.

I feel silly. For wanting to read it. For having it in my bag. Bet I look like a right freak. A right horny freak.

'It's a book.'

'Yeah. I see that.' He laughs, reading the title out loud. '*Miranda Takes a Lover.*'

I try to explain. 'The author.' I point to the photo of her on the blurb. 'She's appearing at the festival, and well, she's pretty mad . . .'

'My nan's got some of her other books at home. I think. I mean, I haven't, like, read any of them before. I just assumed they were like, porn, for old people. I didn't know they were actually good.'

'I just started it today. It's too soon for me to know if it's "good" or not.' I laugh nervously.

He smiles at me when I talk. His eyes on my face.

'What?' I ask, sounding way more confrontational than I meant to.

He shrugs. 'Nothing.'

He flicks through the pages. Not dismissively like I'm half expecting him to. Like I'm expecting him to be as obnoxious as every boy I ever had to share a textbook with at school. He actually looks interested.

Holly and I always read bits of books out loud to each other. Especially sexy bits. But I've never done this with anyone else. Never a *boy*.

I'm determined to not stare at him. But he looks really good. I really want to stare at him. I want to see all of him.

I watch as he flicks through the book, then he turns to the last page.

Oh. My. God.

HE TURNS TO THE VERY LAST PAGE.

No joke. This is not a drill.

HE TURNS

TO THE VERY

LAST

EVER

PAGE IN THE BOOK

AND AS HE STARTS TO READ

HE FOLDS THE BOOK OPEN.

BREAKING THE SPINE.

FOLDING IT IN TWO.

'WHAT ARE YOU DOING?!'

He freezes. 'What?'

'Skipping straight to the last page! That's THE WORST.

It's even sicker than folding the corner of a page instead of using a bookmark or . . . or . . . putting pineapple on a pizza!'

'Mmmm, I love a Hawaiian.' He frowns like he really means it.

Before I can even utter *my only love sprung from my only hate*, he laughs at my outrage. And when he does his eyes nearly disappear. His eyelashes are so long. Oh. GOD.

'I always read the last page first.'

'Whyyyyyyy?!' I whinge, in actual, physical pain now.

'I just like to know what's going to happen.'

This throws me into a spin. Turmoil. HOW can I be attracted to such a MONSTER?

Oh God. *Attracted to?!* What has happened to my very own, very real, ban on romance?

I look out to tiny model Skegton in dismay.

He follows where my eyes have glazed over and places the book back in my bag.

'The pier,' he says.

'Whah?' I blink, waking from my dream.

'That's the pier. It's Skegton's main attraction. They do really good donuts.'

'You like donuts?' I ask, like it's impossible for us to share anything in common now I know he's the kind of psychopath that enjoys fruit on a pizza and book-abuse.

'Who doesn't?' He shrugs.

Well, he has a point.

'I'll show you them. If you want. If you're free and don't have any more fictional animals to dress up as . . .'

I laugh. That kind of awkward, nasal laugh that sounds like nose blowing. 'I mean, I've got a pretty packed afternoon. Y'know, I'm actually wearing a Gruffalo costume under my clothes RIGHT NOW.'

BEST BITS

We walk side by side through the maze of machines in the amusement arcade. There's a western-style shooting range with a dodgy, talking-automaton cowboy, those loud racing-car games, and a couple of small boys going mad for the air hockey table.

Then Robbie says something like, 'Well, even if you're a snob when it comes to reading –'

'Excuse me?!'

'Miss I-Always-Read-A-Book-In-The-Correct-Order...' he mocks.

'Oh my God, it's a basic requirement of reading a book. Or a sentence. Or anything–'

He cuts me off. 'What I was going to say was, *even if you're a snob when it comes to reading*, it's actually pretty fun showing you Skegton-On-Sea's best bits.'

I scoff and shrug and sweat and say something like 'whatever' and watch the carpet as we continue through the arcade, laughing at the stupid names on all the machines. *Greedy Gobs. Viva Las Vegas.* Thinking, *He's having fun, he said he's having fun.*

Then one of the games catches my eye. 'OMG. Look at that!'

It's one of those grabby claw games. It must have been filled with cuddly toys at some point but now all that's left in the Perspex box is one lone cuddly tiger. It looks so sad. Like it's in an enclosure at the zoo. But its plastic eyes are kind of wonky and its legs are all bendy, like if you've ever stuffed a pair of tights with scrunched-up newspaper to make a spider costume.

'Poor guy,' Robbie sympathises.

'All alone in there.'

He starts to dig in the pockets of his black jeans and pulls out a handful of change.

'It's a pound to play . . . I've got about seventy-two p . . .'

'Seriously? You reckon we should actually play?'

My mum always said that those claw grabby things were a con and that nobody ever won on them. They have magnets or something inside so it's impossible to get the prize at all. I've never actually tried it before.

'Don't you? You mean we should leave him? We should carry on with our lives WITHOUT saving him from captivity?'

'Okay, you're right. Let me see what change I have on me.'

Within seconds, my face is pressed up against the glass, unable to believe that Robbie has just clenched the cuddly tiger in the metal claw and it's actually picking it up. I feel like he's clawing at my brain at the same time – those silver talons grasping at my head, and my heart, but there are no magnets or cons to keep me from getting caught.

He holds his breath as the claw returns on autopilot and the cuddly tiger swings dramatically, then plonks into the prize slot.

We both jump up and down with excitement.

I can't believe my eyes. I'm looking at him like he's a flipping freedom-fighting messiah. 'How did you DO that?!' I gush.

'I dunno . . . Seventeen years' worth of practice, I guess!'

We pull the animal out of the flap in the machine. It takes two of us – he's pretty big.

Then Robbie passes him to me. 'He's all yours.'

'No way. I couldn't possibly –'

'Go on. It's a souvenir. A piece of Skegton for you to keep forever and ever.'

'A best bit.'

We decide to call him Barry and parade him around the place triumphantly. It's like I'm in some kind of music-video dream. The kind of cute-couple-having-a-great-time-at-the-fair music video. We lean on a sticky counter-top on the pier waiting for candy floss and donuts. The bloke with the leathery skin and faded tattoos twists his wrist as the pink sugary clouds wind round and round.

My mouth waters. Then my phone rings.

It's Holly.

I motion to Robbie that I'm about to take the call and I take a few steps away from him. Ready to be, like, OHMYGODHOLLYI'MHAVINGTHEBESTANDMOST RANDOMDAY without him hearing.

I slide to answer, my back to the sea. 'Hey, Hol!'

'Paige! This is not a drill. I repeat, this is not a drill! Johnny Hoxton just walked into the shop and he's *PERUSING* the book tent! You have to get back here!'

'What?! OMG!' I squeal. It's not the kind of thing I had planned on doing but it came out of me like a fart in a bubble bath. 'But his event isn't until Friday!'

'He literally just walked past me. He must have been going to one of the events. You need to get here now so we can spy.'

'I'll be there right away!' I say and hang up and look to Robbie, who clearly overheard the whole thing.

'I'll take you there.' He chews on a hot chunk of donut. 'On my bike.'

SCOOTER BOY

Yes, of course he has a scooter because he's that dreamy and he lives by the sea and wears Fred Perry polo shirts. We stomp back along the pier towards town where he says his bike is parked.

I watched *Quadrophenia* late one night at home. It's an old film about mods in the sixties. It made me want to cut my hair into a bob and wear false lashes every day. But mostly it made me want to cling on to boys on mopeds and get off with them in dark alleyways.

Maybe dreams can come true.

My God.

This was not on my list of things to do today but it gets a big fat TICK.

He passes me his helmet. 'Take this.'

I squash my head into it, feeling my cheeks smoosh.

He watches as I clip the strap under my chin and smirks.

'What?' I laugh, no selfie camera mode needed to know just how ridiculous I look.

He shakes his head. 'Nothing.'

Nothing.

Big splodges of rain start to splatter around us. At least this helmet will keep my hair dry.

Robbie's hair is quickly getting soaked. He flicks a lock out of his eyes and I swear real life turns into slo-mo like a Herbal Essences ad.

'Um . . .' I wonder where I should put the huge cuddly tiger. It's pretty much the size of a third person and the moped is pretty small.

'Get on!' he says, perched on the front of the seat.

'I'll just put Barry here.' I squish our stuffed friend between us and clamber onto the back of the bike with zero grace.

'Hang on!'

I wrap my arms around the tiger and touch Robbie's back. I keep my hands in one place. Just touching.

We zoom up the road and I feel like screaming all the way. Luckily I don't. Well, I do a bit, but only when we go around the corners and it feels like we're going to topple over.

We stop at a red light, and as he revs the engine with his right fist I catch our reflection in the window of Argos and I swear this is the sexiest moment of my whole entire life.

Well, it would be, if there wasn't a stuffed safari animal getting in the way of actual, full body contact with the boy of my sun, sea and sand dreams.

Hold on to this, Paige.

Remember this, for when you're an old lady.

This, this is a highlight. A best bit.

In films like *Roman Holiday*, the girl on the back of the bike leans forward and whispers sweet nothings into her lover's ear.

I think I should try this. I mean, *when in Rome, right? Go hard or go home*.

As the lights turn green and we zoom along the high street, I lean forward. Thing is, I'm about ten packs of Birdseye Potato Waffles heavier than Audrey Hepburn and, y'know, Barry's on board . . .

'WHAT?!' He can't hear me over the deafening engine and the rain, so he turns his head.

I feel the bike swerve to one side.

Before I know it we're falling. It feels exactly like a sleep kick, just before you drift off and you feel yourself fall over in bed. But I'm not in bed.

I'm on the cold, wet ground and the moped is on the pavement on the other side of the road.

I soak in the hotel bathtub and the grazes on my knees sting. At least I only came away with grazes. Robbie fractured his ankle.

That's right.

He was taken away in an ambulance.

And his bike. His gorgeous little bike looked kind of mangled on one side. A passer-by who rushed over to help us dragged the bike out of the road and Robbie groaned like the scratches to the moped hurt him more than the impact of his own fall. I limped back to the hotel, Barry the Tiger under my arm, thinking about how I'd managed to pass out inside a pig costume, cause a traffic accident and hospitalise a boy in one day. It goes to show that life outside Greysworth really is more eventful.

Holly knocks on the door.

'Can I come in?'

'Um . . . well . . . I'm kind of naked. Fully naked. Since I'm in the bath and everything . . .' I say, already wrapping my arms around my bare chest even though she's still on the other side of the door.

'But I have so much I want to *ask you* and I don't think

I can wait until you're out of there! I'll cover my eyes and I'll face the wall, I promise.'

She sticks to her end of the deal and demands that I tell her everything.

'It was the most thrilling ten minutes of my life so far . . .' I explain, examining my knee, which is already turning fifty shades of purple before my very eyes. 'But that's it now. I can guarantee I'll never see him again.'

I feel like I'm the reason we crashed and he hurt his leg and messed up his bike. I doubt he's in a mad rush to hang out after that. Which sucks. Because despite my best intentions to cut lads out of my life, I'm pretty sure I like Robbie. I'm actually pretty sure I like him even more than garlic bread and the happy bit at the end of *Dirty Dancing* and those tiny silver balls they use to decorate cakes.

It's like Holly can read my mind, even if she's facing away from me and can't see the dopey grin plastered on my face. 'You fancy him!' she sings. Like we're in Year Six again.

'I do *not*,' I lie. Like I'm in primary school.

'I reckon you've got it bad, Paige,' Holly says to the wall, genuinely chuffed that she's not the only loved-up mug clinging to her phone, waiting for soppy messages to pop up on screen. 'BUT, do you like him even more than Johnny Hoxton?!'

I smirk at my pruny bath fingers.

She continues, 'He was in the bookshop tent for like eight whole minutes and smouldered the whole time. He didn't buy anything, but as he left, he looked at me and he said, "Thank you." Thank you! He's even more gorgeous in real life. You have to be there next time!'

'I *have* to!' I splash some tepid water at the back of her head. 'Now, turn away! The water's cold, I'm coming out!'

LiTTLE dEATHS

My bruised knees crack as I arrange a pile of novels into a pyramid shape. My legs are killing me today. That's the small price I'll pay for flinging myself off a moving moped.

Holly takes my mind off it by doing the *best* impression of Minnie, flouncing around the signing tent, granny-donated scarf slung around her shoulders. 'True love comes in all shapes and sizes. I rather love the size of my big-huge-hefty chair!' she scoffs as she sinks into Lady Rockwell's gilded throne.

I pick a flower from one of the giant vases and put on my poshest voice to sigh, 'Ahhhh, the lily. Flower of death.'

I twirl and cackle and all of a sudden spot the fuchsia apparition that is Minnie Rockwell, standing right beside me. Where did she *come* from?!

I stumble and fall. Pulling on the lace tablecloth to save

me, I manage to knock Minnie's vase of pink lilies over and onto the floor.

'Follicles!' I hiss. *Follicles* is a word I use to replace *bollocks* with at work, so that Tony can't give me a *follicking* for swearing on duty.

'The flower of death, indeed,' Minnie announces, eyes wide. Crap. She totally heard us.

'I'm so sorry!' I blabber, scrambling on the floor in a pathetic attempt to salvage the flowers. They're all crushed and bent out of shape. My knees click, still feeling tender after yesterday's traffic accident.

Minnie continues as if I haven't said anything at all. 'You know, my third husband was a Frenchman.' Her eyes sparkle beneath the eye shadow and tarantula-like lashes. '*La petite mort.*'

Holly looks at me, then back to the soggy carpet, trying very hard to suppress an eruption of giggles.

'Do you know what that means, girls?' She doesn't wait for us to answer. 'The direct translation is *little death*. To reach one's *destination* . . . in the throes of love . . . can feel like a little death indeed.'

Is she saying what I think she's saying?

I force eye contact with Holly, who confirms my suspicions by mouthing ORGASM silently.

'That is why I always *love* to be surrounded by pink lilies. By all of those little deaths,' Minnie warbles.

'I'm so sorry about the lilies,' I repeat.

'That's quite all right, my dear girl. You may fetch me some fresh ones.' She smiles and breezes out of the room in a pink cloud of perfume and dog hair.

Fetch her some fresh flowers?

Fetch?! Like I'm a dog. Like I'm *her* dog? Bet that dog's never had to fetch anything in its entire life. All it does is sit there looking all sad and freaky in *Dame Lady Rockwell whatever's* lap.

I have no idea where I'm supposed to find any pink lilies in Skegton-On-Sea anyway, but before I know it, I'm out and pounding the high street, fuming at myself for getting caught dicking around, and for being told to *fetch* something and then actually doing it anyway. Who knows what festival goodness I'm missing while I'm on this complete waste of a mission?! What if JOHNNY HOXTON makes another appearance in my absence? I don't need some jumped-up pantomime dame making my Fear of Missing Out syndrome worse than it already is.

I make do with two bouquets from the doorway of Tesco Express. I'll pick out the lilies and ditch the yellow wilted bits that look like throwing them on the floor would actually make them look better than they currently do.

I can feel the scabs on my knees sticking to my black tights. Yesterday's moped wounds are bleeding. I hobble into Superdrug in search of plasters. I could get the manky beige ones that go all grey and bobbly around the edges . . . but I choose the sparkly Hello Kitty ones instead.

I check my reflection in the Rimmel make-up display. Careful not to re-squash the new flowers in one arm, I'm drawn to a bright pink lipstick. I pick it up, pull off the shiny lid. It's brighter than any colour I have in my own collection, but I try it on. Right there in the shop. Not the tester though, because I'm not a complete tramp. I pucker my lips and pout in the grimy mirror.

'*Fetch this!*' I say to nobody in particular.

After paying for my Big Girl plasters and lippy, I head back to the festival.

I pass Robbie's nan's souvenir shop. It's on my way, really; it's not as if I'm stalking him or anything. He's probably already arranged a restraining order against me for pulling him off his bike and breaking his ankle.

As I pass the shop I glance over and see his nan. She's tying the nets of beach balls and sandcastle-shaped buckets to the awning, and she's having to reach up really high above her head to do it. I guess that's usually Robbie's job. With him being so tall and that.

Maybe his injuries are worse than I thought. Maybe he can't even walk any more.

Oh God, what if he didn't pull through?! The loss of his beloved bike may have been too much and his heart might have stopped beating.

And I was there, in those final moments of his life.

And I was the silly cow who ended his life by attempting to live out some cinematic fantasy on him. What have I done?!

A big gust of wind blows a flimsy yellow plastic spade over Robbie's nan's shoulder, towards me.

She looks at me and frowns. Oh God, I wish I could just scuttle away with my flowers and lipstick, just disappear into the cracks in the promenade. Instead I cradle Minnie's flowers in one arm and bend down (which really hurts my dodgy knees, by the way) and pass the little spade back to her.

'Thank you, love.'

Okay, cool, so she's not slapped me round the face with it, like I half expected her to. It's what I would do to somebody if I suspected them of killing *my* grandson.

'How's Robbie?' I whisper, just in case it really is bad news.

I'm ready to apologise profusely, to hand over Minnie Rockwell's lilies as a sign of my sincerest condolences when she puts her hands on her hips and says, 'Robbie? That little beggar's grounded! How many times have I told him how dangerous that bloody bike is?! He says he'll be working all hours around the clock to save up so he can repair it – well, at least when he's here I can keep an eye on him!' She shakes her head. 'You weren't hurt were you, pet?'

'Oh, no! I'm just . . . I'm glad he's okay.'

'All right, Paige?' Robbie hobbles out of the shop door and leans on a rack of postcards.

Wow. He's the first person to make crutches look fit.

'You shouldn't have.' He nods at the bouquet of flowers in my arms and grins. 'My nan might have grounded me but I'm not *dead*.'

I am so, so glad he's not dead.

His nan laughs and swipes at him with a Skegton-On-Sea tea towel. 'Get inside that shop and sell some souvenirs, you!'

'I should get back, anyway . . .' I murmur as I turn away from their family business.

'It looks good on you, by the way.' Robbie stops and smiles at me.

I don't know what he's on about.

'The lipstick.'

I feel my cheeks turn the same shade of fuchsia as my gob. 'Thank you.'

I trip back to the festival, clutching Minnie's lilies, feeling like I just DIED right there and then.

Julius

Holly is a full six months older than me.

She doesn't do it so much these days, but when we were younger, she loved to remind me of the age gap. Like when we were trying to settle disagreements (usually disputes along the lines of 'How long are baby hamsters bald before they get fluffy?' or 'Is this particular member of a boyband gay?') she'd posture about being the oldest, and therefore the wisest.

Holly's birthday is tomorrow, so technically she's turning seventeen when the clock strikes twelve tonight. Seventeen suddenly seems well old. Especially, seventeen *with a boyfriend.* An actual, real-life, breathing boyfriend. As opposed to the imaginary one we concocted on the walk home from school a few years ago. He was a perfect mixture of the cute boy, Dean, who worked in Costa, and the punky lad we saw on a school trip to London and had lusted over for months since.

Now that the lilies are back to where they should be, I restock paper bags behind the bookshop tent counter.

Holly pouts into her selfie camera. 'You know what? I seriously think I'm already ageing . . .'

I frown. 'Do not be ridiculous.'

'No! I'm not complaining! I like it. I think I'm starting to look more like . . . *me* . . .'

I stare at her, waiting for a response. She literally looks exactly the same as she has done for the past three years, since the only major alteration: brace removal.

'I can't believe this is my last day of living my life as a sixteen year old . . .'

This girl is so dramatic. Does she really think her world will be turned upside-down when she wakes up under her Sea View Lodge duvet tomorrow? She's fuelling the fire that makes all adults pat you on the arm and ask you 'how it feels' on your birthday. I never knew what to say to that. I'd just shrug and think, *I dunno, I'm eleven*.

Holly flutters her eyelashes into the camera lens before hunching over her phone, tapping at the screen with her thumbs. I hear the little *whoooosh* pop sound when her selfie sends to Jamie. Then a buzz reply.

'Okay, Jamie says I have to make sure I'm around to FaceTime him at midnight so he can wish me a LIVE happy birthday . . .'

'That's really cute.' I smile. And y'know, it *is* really cute but obvs I was going to be doing the majority of midnight birthday wishing, as I do *every year*, so Jamie isn't such an innovator or anything . . .

'I'm soooo excited, Paige! My birthday! At the Skegton Book Festival!' She grinds her teeth into a manic grin and it's infectious; I'm gurning away like a nutter too when Tim bounces over. His long, smooth ponytail swishes side to side as he walks, kind of just like the netball girls at school. Shiny hair does that. Not frizzy hair like mine. Not that I ever wanted to swish like the netball girls; I thought they looked like some kind of weird cult, bounding around in those florescent bibs, hair moving the same way at the same time. I laughed at them, but Tim's different. Tim's all right actually. Tim's –

TIM'S HOLDING MY SKETCHBOOK.

RED ALERT! RED ALERT!

VERY private property, containing private sketches, thoughts, EMOTIONS – in the hands of a semi-stranger! What the hell?! I must have left it out of my bag by mistake.

'I believe this is yours . . .'

I grab it out of his hands faster than if he was holding a hot cheese and onion pasty from Greggs.

It's so dumb of me to just leave it lying around! I don't even need to *look* at Holly to know she's cringing at the severity of the situation. She was, after all, the one who stood in the toilet cubicle next to mine, flushing the chain repeatedly to drown out the sound of my crying on the neighbouring loo, after a group of Year Eleven girls had sifted through my GCSE portfolio and said, 'It's pretty good, for a Year Ten.' *Good, for a Year Ten.* Those words swarmed around in my head like a million annoying bluebottle flies. It hurt as much as somebody saying, 'You're not bad . . . *for a girl.*' Like they're making an allowance for you being less than, because their expectations are so low to begin with. Yuck! EUGH!

The life-drawing class me and Holly joined has defo helped how I feel about sharing my work, and I'm not *as* protective over it as I used to be . . . but still . . . all I can think about, as Tim rubs his now-empty hands together, is that I had multiple sketches of Robbie in this book. Drawn from memory, not observation. I know that they'd be way better if they were done with him right there in front of me.

Which he'll probably never be, because, y'know, he's *grounded*.

It's kind of cringe that he's grounded. My mum never did that to us. I mean, there's not really anywhere to *go* in Greysworth, so forcing me to stay at home, where I have books and telly and don't have to wear a bra, doesn't really seem like punishment at all. If she'd made me 'play out' with some of the swishy netball girls then that would have made me behave myself forever and ever, amen.

BUT OH GOD ANYWAY what am I doing drawing memory sketches of some random, grounded, *gorgeous* BOY?! I came to this town determined to remain un-muddled by matters of the heart, and now look at me . . . I blame all of this on the romance crap Minnie Rockwell is peddling . . .

'Ah . . . they've arrived!' Tim points to the big, flat, DO NOT BEND packages that were delivered to the tent by a man wearing shorts with lots of pockets and one of those little hand-held signature computer thingies.

'What's inside that?' I ask.

'It should be . . . a life-sized Julius . . .' Tim grunts as he wrestles with the TEAR ALONG THIS LINE tabs.

Me and Holly frown at each other. What the fudge is a life-sized Julius?!

As he peels back the brown corrugated card, Tim reveals a cutout of a man who looks exactly like the bloke on all of Minnie's covers.

'So, the guy on all of these books is an actual person?' Holly asks, studying the front of a novel and holding it up to our new 2D mate in comparison. It's the one called *Clarissa's Highland Fling*. It depicts his shiny bare chest bursting out of an open, billowing shirt. His hair is long and straight, and, in keeping with this novel's Scottish theme, he's wearing a kilt. In other books, he's a pirate, and a 'rogue' and all sorts of other babe characters to fulfil the dreams of every sort of reader.

'Yeah, he's kind of a big deal to Lady Rockwell fans,' Tim explains. 'He's called Julius.'

'Just Julius?' I ask, ready to Google the phenomenon.

'Yeah. Like Madonna.'

'Or Terry from Terry's Chocolate Oranges,' Holly offers.

'Is Julius coming here? To Skegton?' I ask, kind of weirded-out by his shiny pecs and receding hairline, now leaning against our trestle table.

'No, we couldn't get him. He lives in LA. Good thing we've got these instead.' Tim laughs and props one of the cutouts beside the bookshop tent door.

'Oh wow . . . Julius had a brief music career back in the day!' I chuckle as my phone loads a YouTube clip of Julius performing on an ancient episode of *Top of the Pops*. '*In at number nineteen, it's a new entry for Julius with "Love Ain't Blind" . . .'*

'Speaking of pop stars . . . I know you two are Johnny Hoxton fans . . .'

Holly jumps to her feet, and I silence the crap song blaring out of my phone. Turner and Maguire, reporting for fangirl duty.

'So are you going to the gig he's doing tonight?'

'Ex-ca-yuse me?!' My jaw drops. It dislocates.

Tim stands with his hands on his hips, loving the fact that he's the one breaking this HOT SLICE OF STUFFED-CRUST GOSS to us. 'His band . . . y'know, his old band . . . broken up now . . . what were they called?'

'VELVET LULLABY.' We both say it at the same time, obviously.

'Well . . . they're not actually re-forming but Johnny Hoxton *apparently* is doing an acoustic set of their old stuff. At the Tarantula. It's a club down on the pier.'

'WELL THAT'S IT WE'RE GOING.' I shrug. Simple really.

'I'm pretty sure it's sold out. They were giving away wristbands at HMV. You need one to get in.'

Before we hold a minute's silence for the Greysworth branch of HMV that closed down last year (just weeks after I was refused a 15 certificate DVD by a member of staff. My younger brother *still* won't let me live that down ...) can I just CRY about the fact that we've only just found out about this secret gig? How were we supposed to know about the wristbands?

I wish I'd known about this sooner. It would have been the BEST BIRTHDAY PRESENT EVER. The pressie I have instead of a Johnny Hoxton wristband seems really measly now. It's a cake candle in the shape of a lamb. Holly loves lambs. I think it's meant to be for Easter cakes but screw the societal pressures forced upon young girls dictating which candles we should and shouldn't burn at specific times of year. Smash the patriarchy NOW!

I also picked up one of the rude pens from the souvenir shop. It's a blue Biro with a picture of a man in shorts on the side, but when you turn it upside down, the water in the pen erases the shorts and you actually see the man's actual penis. I cracked myself up with this present, and had already flashed forward to the look on Monique's FACE when Holly pulls it out of her pencil case in French next term ... but now, knowing that Johnny Hoxton GIG ENTRY was a thing, that craps all over my happy present parade.

Dammit!

'What kind of place is Tarantula, Tim?'

He laughs, 'Well, it's not somewhere I frequent, I must say! I'm more of a real ale man myself . . . It's a nightclub.'

'Well, we could try getting in?' I offer.

'We don't have any ID,' Holly sulks. And she's right. As I said, that instance of DVD-shaped humiliation in HMV is still at the forefront of my mind and stops me from buying scratch cards when I'm feeling lucky, let alone sneaking my way into clubs named after spiders.

Minnie Rockwell breezes into the bookshop tent and places a liver-spotted hand on Julius's chest, all of the gems on her rings dazzling in the temporary, fluorescent strip lights. 'Oh, Julius, darling, you're looking good.' She leans over and kisses the cardboard cutout ON THE LIPS. The flat, non-existent lips! She cackles and winks at Tim. God, she really must be losing the plot.

KISSING KEN

The countdown to Holly's Official Midnight Birthday is ON. We're in our room, telly glowing, and have demolished three of those tear'n'share bags of Revels. Holly's left all of the raisin ones in the packets, but I don't mind them so I hoover them up in my mouth.

'We should have got a cucumber for our eyes! Like in films . . .' I suggest, wiggling my metallic Barry M toes on the chintzy hotel bedspread.

Holly isn't paying full attention to me. She's giggling at her phone. At Jamie. Eye roll.

I'm pretty certain they're getting it on. I can't help but feel left behind. Like when Alison McGarvey announced out of the blue that she didn't like playing with Barbies any more. She said they were for little kids and boring. I was soooo not over Barbie at that stage. All I wanted to do was plait her multicoloured hair and make her snog the one token Ken doll (who was getting around a bit, TBH, hooking up with every babe in my toy collection, the love rat).

Well, now it's not Barbies who are snogging. It's real-life people. My real-life best friend and her real-life boy. And, well, what about me?

It started with Holly telling me every little detail. She'd message me screen shots of their back and forth text convos and we'd discuss it in full. Sometimes she'd even ask me what she should reply back. But then, after a while, she developed more loyalty towards Jamie, which I guess is normal and everything . . . but it means that she doesn't show and tell me all the little stories any more . . . I'm just here, wigglin' my toes and banging on about cucumber.

'Hol . . .'

Something in my tone, which I know came out a bit whinier than expected, makes her put her phone down and look over at me.

'Next week we'll be back in Greysworth, back in the common room scrapping around for a pair of wheelie chairs that aren't broken . . .'

'Such a rarity . . .'

'Right?! And we'll be bored out of our minds, just

thinking about how we came SO CLOSE to seeing Johnny Hoxton perform tonight. We're in the same town he's playing in. How mad is that?! They're calling it an INTIMATE gig! Holly, this could be our chance to see him INTIMATELY.'

'Gaaaaaah! You're right! Okay. Yes – what are we doing sitting here in our pyjamas?! Tonight I turn SEVENTEEN! We should start as we mean to go on! Let's turn up and TRY to get into the venue at least!' She jumps off the bed and bounces around on the patterned carpet. 'Oh, but promise we'll be free at midnight? For Jamie?'

'Cross my heart, hope to die, stick a poodle in my eye.'

I run to the bathroom and whip my retainer out of my gob faster than you can say *SEASIDE HEARTTHROB FREE GIG MY GOD.*

BiRTHdAY BUMPS

The only times I ever read magazines is when they get ditched in the common room at college. They can be a pretty LOL source of entertainment on a slow day in Sixth Form. Problem pages and tips on how to 'please your man' and guides on how to turn your daytime look into your nighttime look. Well, me and Holly scrambled around our hotel room turning our PJ look into our Yes-I-Swear-I-Am-Eighteen-Please-Allow-Me-Into-Your-Establishment look. Once I read something about curly hair making you look younger than straight hair, so you can betcha me and Hol were there in front of the mirror, running GHDs over our fringes until we felt we looked mature enough to hit the town.

Foolishly, I didn't pack going out clothes. Since I don't go out at home, I expected this trip to be the same, but

I've never been happier to say I was wrong! Holly packed everything she owns so I wriggled into one of her dresses – black with tiny sequins all over it – and put it with black tights and DMs, natch.

We're feeling pretty GORGE as we head out, only for the wet mist coming off the sea to spray our hair and flick my fringe skywards as we find our way to the Tarantula bar.

There's a queue of people lined up by the door.

We wait. And we wait some more. And we still hang around as the bouncer tells the group of people who are at least ten places in front of us that the club has reached full capacity so it's strictly a one-in-one-out policy.

Nobody in their right mind would leave a Johnny Hoxton gig once they'd made it in there.

I hear the opening bars to 'My Baby You' strumming in the background. It pulls my heart apart like the Incredible Hulk's little T-shirt.

'C'mon, Paige! It's nearly midnight!' Holly tugs at my sleeve, frowning in the glow of her phone.

But – the queue . . . and the waiting . . . I've actually resigned myself to the fact that I may never even *need* to fake losing my imaginary driving license but . . . it feels like we're so near. Johnny Hoxton is just on the other side of that huge bloke with the puffer jacket and radio! I know I should respect the Birthday Girl's wishes though . . .

'Haha! All right Cinderella, keep your slippers on!'

'The signal's crap down here! Quick, let's get back towards the hotel!'

I slow down to get a look at Robbie's shop. The lights are all off. Obviously. As if there's ever going to be a mad rush for rock and multicoloured sand at midnight in Skegton.

Holly yanks my arm. 'Paige! I said come *on* –'

And it happens. Almost like it's happening in slow motion.

Holly's phone tumbles out of her hand and falls, falls, falls.

We both slump to our knees to try to save it. Like at this very moment in my life, I'll have finally been granted the gift of hand-eye coordination.

The iPhone drops. It's going to smash, oh God it's going to smash to pieces on the wooden boardwalk of the pier. OH GOD, EVEN WORSE.

It slides straight through a gap in the pier. Between the wooden beams of the pier. It drops through the gap and into the sea below us.

I think I scream. Holly is definitely screaming – that slow-motion low-pitch wail that happens in films. I'm just holding her. That phone, and her midnight birthday wish from Jamie, are long gone.

'I'm so sorry,' I whisper. The sound of the waves crashing beneath us becomes the only sound. Holly sniffs, wipes her eyes with sleeves pulled over her fists.

'All of my photos . . . of us and the festival and . . . my nan . . .' her voice wavers, 'and *Jamie* . . . they're all *gone* . . .' She kneels in the dark, staring down into the sea. 'This is the worst birthday ever.' She sobs, her chin all wobbly and dimpled like a buttered crumpet. 'It's even worse than the year I cracked my head open at that laser tag place.'

I wince, remembering the carnage unfurl amidst the caterpillar cake and party bags to that cringy dubstep soundtrack.

I feel really crap and wholly responsible for Holly's disappointment right now. 'I think I know something that'll make you feel better . . .'

The proper fish'n'chip shop chippies are closed now. It's too late. There's a takeaway glowing in the foggy night sky. KEV-BAB. I take that to be a mixture of Kevin and kebab. Adam at Bennett's told me that when you push two words together to make a new one like that it's called a portmanteau. I hope the kebabs aren't actually made from Kevin's body parts.

'I'll just have chips.'

Holly's quiet. I hate that she's having a bad time, but it's a well-known fact that chips make everything better. These chips come in small orange cardboard boxes that say *DELICIOUS CHICKEN* on the lid. There's little paper sachets of salt. I empty three of them onto my chips. And while Holly zigzags ketchup all over hers, I plop a big dollop of mysteriously pink 'burger sauce' into the corner of mine.

We perch on the vinyl bar stools by the wall and I catch my reflection in the mirrored tiles. So much for straight and sophisticated locks. My hair is living its best life in thirteen different directions. Holly's cheeks are still a little bit puffy from the crying. It breaks my heart to see her sniffle – it's that delayed sniffle that still creeps up on you up to twenty minutes after you've finished emotionally letting rip.

'Holly, look at the time!' I point to the big clock on the wall. 'Happy birthday! Officially.' We hug and I pull her present out of my bag. I wrapped it in this cool iridescent paper from Paperchase that is giving us pink and silver and green under the bright lights of the kebab shop.

'Oh my God, Paige! A little lamb!' She smiles, eyes still watery.

'A birthday lamb.'

'This is so cute . . .'

I stick the lamb candle into her box of chips. It really is a beautiful sight to behold. She claps her hands together and when I start singing 'Happy Birthday', the men in aprons behind the counter join in, one of them reaching over with a lighter to light the candle.

'Make a wish!'

She blows out her candle and stuffs a chip in her mouth.

'Take my phone, Hol. It doesn't have FaceTime but if you know Jamie's number, call him. I don't need all my minutes this month.'

She squeezes me and taps the keypad with her greasy, chippy hands. I don't even mind when she slopes outside of the shop to make the call, I'm just happy that at the start of her seventeenth birthday, my best friend in the world gets to chat to the boy whose number she's memorised by heart.

LoVE LETTeRS

Minnie Rockwell is the poshest person I've ever met.

I mean, you'd have to be posh to pull off a name like Minnie, wouldn't you? You can't be called Minnie and not be posh. Or a Disney character. Also, after only a few days in her company, I've heard her say 'sensational' many, many times. And it's the *way* she pronounces it: '*Sen-SAY-tional!*' Bet everything in Lady Rockwell's world is sensational.

This is what I'm thinking as I slump on a plastic chair, slipping Skegton-On-Sea Book Fest bookmarks into the title pages of every Minnie Rockwell book, ready for her to sign.

She's already been here for hours, longing out the process of scribbling her name on the same page, in the same way, over and over again. Everything she does is a performance. I've zoned out TBH. I've just been distracting myself with the memory of Robbie reading the last page of that book until Holly taps me on the shoulder.

I know I joked about her waking up on her seventeenth birthday and feeling transformed, but she really is surprisingly bright eyed and bushy tailed today, despite last night's disaster. I said she could share my phone to text Jamie and call her mum (to thank her for giving birth seventeen years ago). Let's face it, the most exciting text I can expect to get all week will probs be a message from EE telling me I've reached my data allowance. Hot stuff.

When we arrived at the festival this morning, Penny presented Holly with a salted caramel birthday brownie (which Holly shared with me, even though I had already abused the breakfast bar at our hotel by scoffing three fried eggs and about six hash browns. A buffet will always get the better of me. I'm lucky to have such a supportive friend who will enable this behaviour). Holly's been given a clipboard and looks very official. It's funny how a clipboard can really give someone a sense of authority. She's tied her hair up into a neat little bun on top of her head. I feel like I want to ask her for information, like she must know EVERYTHING, despite the fact that I saw her dribble toothpaste on her jeans this morning. She pulls up the chair next to me and whispers about having ten minutes before she has to be on the door for an event.

Penny's given Holly all the big responsibilities. Being on the door for things is not a task I've been saddled with, probably down to the fact Holly has remained conscious throughout the festival so far, and hasn't inflicted bodily harm on any of the locals. Yet. I mean, there's still time.

She helps me stuff the books and we both fall silent, listening in to Minnie's monologue.

Geraldine sits quietly while Minnie runs through the outfits she's packed for her trip. This is when she mentions a letter-writing dress and the dress she wears for eating lunch at home.

Holly nudges me and whispers, 'OMG I wish *I* had an outfit designated for eating lunch at home!'

'I kind of do. It's not as glam as I suspect hers is though.'

It's period-stained pyjama bottoms and an ancient One Direction T-shirt. FYI, the 1D tee was originally purchased for pure ironic jokes, but has somehow worked its way into my Most Worn, if only in the comfort of my own home.

I'm so fascinated by Minnie that I've started Googling her. Unashamedly. Sometimes even in the same room as her. She'll only be a few high-heeled trots away and I'm watching an interview with her on my phone, one headphone not-so-discreetly to my ear. I guess I just had no idea how famous she was before I met her. I had no idea that she was the Queen of Romance or that she had written *hundreds* of books in her time.

I've seen pictures of her at her big country manor house. It looks really fancy, like everything inside it would fetch a bomb on *Antiques Roadshow*.

And her fans are, like, proper die-hard fans. I've seen a few of them approach her already, clutching well-loved editions of her books.

'Would you like to hear today's letters, Ms Rockwell?' Geraldine offers, in a voice so soft you could serve it in a wafer cone with sticky raspberry sauce on top.

'Oh, good *idea*, Geraldine! Yes, read them out to me. We don't want to fall behind now do we?'

Minnie bats her lashes at me and beckons me over to where she's reclining. 'Miss Turner . . .'

Seriously. *Miss Turner?!*

'I'm going to need some assistance with my fan correspondence . . .'

I blink, and I panic, unsure of what this has to do with me.

'Would you be so kind as to help me with penning my replies?'

'Oh, yes! Of course!'

I scramble around behind the counter and come up with a Bic Biro and a pad of lined paper.

'There you go!' I watch her, watching me. She's bewildered. It's like I've just suggested the most ridiculous thing in the world. Like I've just crouched down beside her and asked if she can have a crack at squeezing the spots on my back that I can't reach or something.

She lowers her voice and smiles, as if she's giving me some friendly advice. 'Just take a seat beside me, my dear. Geraldine will read the fan mail, then I shall dictate a reply and you will write it up for me.'

Right then.

Do I actually get a say in this? I guess not!

Holly grimace-laughs and waves at me with her clipboard before creeping out of the tent, so she can, y'know, take part in something that's actually book-festival related! I feel like I'm stuck in the classroom at lunchtime writing lines while my friends run around eating Dairylea Dunkers in the playground.

I've always been moderately well behaved at school. I've only had to write lines once and it was for a very minor offence – laughing at the lads who kept interrupting our Music lesson by hitting the demo buttons on the keyboards.

It drove Mr Webb INSANE and it was pretty funny at the time. It was also the reason we were banned from touching any instruments during Music lessons for the rest of the year. You've never truly known eye-watering kill-me-now-boredom until you've spent a whole term on a comprehension exercise about synthesisers.

I open the notepad to the first clear page and siiiigh, waiting for Minnie to start dictating. This is NOT what I signed up for.

'Now,' Minnie explains, through closed eyelids. Isn't it funny when people do that? When they talk to you with their eyes shut? I do not understand this woman. 'Geraldine doesn't usually deal with my letters. I have a separate secretary for this, on account of there being so many, but I don't want to build up a backlog while I'm away . . .' She pets the snotty little dog on her lap.

'Do you get a lot of letters?' I ask, genuinely curious.

'Oh yes, hundreds of letters from fans, and I respond to them all.'

'What kind of things do they write to you about?' I doodle on the margin of my page as I look at Minnie. It's very hard to draw her without it looking like a caricature. I cross my legs and hold the pad upright, to make sure she can't see what I'm up to.

'Well, they tell me about the books. How they make them feel . . .' Minnie explains. 'Many women live lives and feel like they've never been listened to, never been understood – by husbands, children . . . society. I've had women explain to me that they've read something in one of my books and it has felt for them like somebody finally said the thing they couldn't bear to say to themselves . . . I get letters from men too, of course . . .' She groans. 'Oh, and there was *The Wild Heart of Eloise*. I had so many complaints about the ending – in which Eloise left her lover – that I rewrote it and that version was republished. If you have one of the first editions today it'll fetch a few hundred pounds on the internet.'

'Wow, so you mean you actually changed the ending for your fans?'

'Well, it's all for them, isn't it? They are the paying customers after all.' She shrugs – all shoulder pads and sparkly diamantés – and bats her thick black lashes at me.

'Cool . . .'

'Let's begin, Geraldine.' She smiles, and revels in the messages from her adoring fans. Minnie is certainly someone who can take a compliment. Nobody I know is like that. All the girls at school just automatically reject any nice thing they're told about themselves. Like if someone says, 'Wow, your hair looks nice,' it's as if they're expected to go, 'Oh *God*, no, it's a total mess – I need to wash it!' Minnie is the complete opposite. In fact, it's as if she's bathing in the warmth of these letters. Soaking in the joy, letting herself have that luxury like it's a big Lush bubble bath. It's cool – it's way better than pretending you don't know you're IT.

I make sure to do my best, neatest handwriting for these letters. Way more attention to detail than if these were lines for dicky Mr Webb. There's a Lady Rockwell fan called Barbara and I'm particularly proud of the way I write the big loopy *B* at the top of the letter. It looks like it's snapped from one of those brush pen Instagram accounts.

It takes all my tongue-out concentration, and before I know it, hundreds of people are piling into the bookshop tent, picking up the same book, and heading for the till. The event Holly was working at must have finished.

I ditch the pen and paper and excuse myself, before getting buried alive in a mountain of arms and contactless payments and paper bags and people who pay and then decide that actually they don't need four copies of the same book THEY NEED FIVE, oh great, yes, sure, no problem. That'll be ten ninety-nine, please. Bags are free of charge. Free bags. No you don't need to pay for bags. Thank you thank you thank you.

I'm so hot and bothered that my red lit-fest T-shirt is clinging to me and my eyebrows feel like they're sliding right down my forehead.

Where's Holly? I could do with some help here. These festival-goers are relentless.

Over the initial gaggle of people crowding the till waving twenty-pound notes at me like I'm some kind of *stripper*, I sense some commotion in the distance.

It's Minnie. She's lifting that dog off the carpet and holding it up in the air like the 'Circle of Life' bit in *The Lion King*.

'Whoopsie daisy! Has *somebody* had an accident?'

WOOF

'*Excuse* me!' A customer with small rectangular glasses and a big scarf points a rolled-up festival programme to a spot on the carpet. 'You'll need to clean that up straight away!'

I move through the crowds to see it.

A fresh dollop of dog poo on the carpet.

'Let's take you outside – come-come, there we are!' Minnie's upped and left with that mongrel, and I'm stood here, surrounded by people who want to see me pick this crap up.

Oh God. If Penny comes back to this chaos then she'll think I'm incapable of looking after the bookshop by myself. I'll never be trusted with a clipboard.

Okay then. I've never done this before . . . I pick up an empty Kettle Chips packet. This'll do. Sure, I'll never look at Seasalt and Cracked Black Pepper flavour in the same way again, but it'll do.

How can such a small THING produce this much crap?! It's vile. Kind of not really a liquid or a solid. It looks a bit like peanut butter. Crunchy peanut butter.

It's ruining my LIFE.

This is NOT what I signed up for.

Let's just accept the fact that THIS IS NOT WHAT I SIGNED UP FOR will be etched onto my headstone when I die. I'll probably die here, in Skegton, from whatever next task Minnie decides she needs me for. I'll die, having never laid eyes on Johnny Hoxton, and never seeing Robbie again.

Surely this is a violation of my human rights.

'Make way! Make way! Coming through!'

The festival-goers part like the Red Sea as I stride, crisp packet of poo in my outstretched hand, out of the door and over to the wheelie bins outside. It's wet and muddy out here. I just want rid of this thing but I have to walk as though *I'm* the one who's soiled myself, just to avoid slipping right over in the slush.

I spoke too soon. Before I know it, I'm down on one knee, like I'm proposing – with a *horrible* alternative to an engagement ring.

'Paige? Paige!' Holly and Tim dash over to me. I'm still here, lunging in the dirt *with* the dirt.

All I can say is, 'Please help me up.'

Seeing as this is a festival after all, there are no real toilets. We have Portaloos instead. They're not like the blue box ones you see on building sights, and they're not like the ones Hannah Lambert told us they had at Reading Festival. (She told us a horror story about how a boy got tipped over inside one and emerged covered in other people's crap.) These ones seem like they're a step up from your average festival loo and look a bit like the Portakabin classrooms we had at primary school, but funnily enough they smell less like toilets than Year Four did.

I wash my hands thoroughly in the little yellow sink and recoil in horror at my reflection in the mirror. I'd look cute if it wasn't for the blue Biro ink on my chin and the blobby bits of mascara in the corners of my eyes. I look exhausted. I feel it too.

After I've scrubbed my hands to what I reckon is a surgical standard of clean, I notice that we're out of paper towels. I squash into the miniature cubicle and bend to reach for some toilet roll. My bag slips off my shoulder and its contents tumble down the loo. Could this day get any worse? Yes. Apparently it could. The toilet gurgles and starts flushing itself! NO!

I press the little button on the wall in a vain effort to make it stop, but it just makes a load of extra water gush around the bowl and swirl my belongings further down.

FFS!

In go my surgically clean hands. I grab my bank card, my keys. I fish out my pink fountain pen. It's the best pen I've ever had. Saved, but at what cost? Oh my God just think of all the bums that have sat on this toilet. NO!

I pull my hands out and stand to watch the liquid eyeliner I bought just last week and the Nero's card (that OMG was only TWO stamps away from a free drink) slip away from me. Gone forever.

I'm back at the sink, pounding the soap dispenser furiously.

'Skegton Book Festival will not break me. Skegton Book Festival will not break me. Skegton Book Festival will not –'

Without thinking, I reach for the empty paper towel basket again. I pat my hands dry on my legs and storm out of the Portaloos.

I get back to the bookshop tent, only to find Minnie and

that INCONTINENT DOG still hanging around. 'Paige, there's just one more thing . . .'

I feel my head explode. And then I explode.

'Oh, *is there*, Minnie?! Anything else I can do for you? Any more lilies you want me to "fetch" or something you want me to lick off the carpet? Any more lives you'd like me to RUIN while I'm at it? Why do you need Geraldine here if you're just going to order me about instead?' Geraldine folds her arms at me. 'No offence, Geraldine, I'm just not really clear on who is expected to do EVERYTHING for Minnie Rockwell any more.'

Minnie raises a pencilled-in eyebrow and warbles, 'Geraldine is my secretary. She's here making notes as I come up with my latest piece, *A Woman on the Edge of Love*.'

Oh Goddddddddddddd. I'll show her a woman on the edge. That's it. 'You know what, Minnie, I've had enough. I'm not your skivvy!'

The pearlescent blue on her eyelids disappears. Her eyes are wide, staring at me. Then she cackles. She actually fully cackles in my face.

Holly appears by my side, touching my arm, trying to settle me down.

But why is Minnie Rockwell laughing at me? It doesn't

make me angrier like it should. It just confuses me. Oh God, she's GOOD.

'Yours.' Minnie hands me the lined notebook I was using for letter writing. 'Thank you for the portrait. It shows a great likeness.'

I flip the page to see the sketches I made of her, sketches she must have seen. Crap.

She picks her dog up in her claw-like hands and leaves the tent with Geraldine by her side.

I turn to Holly, who is officially gobsmacked. 'Whoah. That's all I can say, Paige. Just whoah.'

LADDER CULTURE

I stomp into the tent they're setting up for Minnie's next event under a massive crate of Rockwell novels needed here for display.

I still feel kind of awkward around her after everything I said to her earlier. It was really intense, and really unprofessional. If Penny had seen that I don't know what would have happened. I wonder if it'll get back to Tony in Greysworth. I hope not. I'd be stuck on dusting duty and taking out the bins for the rest of my short career at Bennett's if he only knew.

I don't know how I'll ever clear the air with someone like Minnie. Maybe we can just avoid each other from now on. It's not like I came here to see her or anything. I'll just drop this box of books here, then get back to the shop tent to mind my own beeswax.

Looks like this place is nearly ready for her talk. There are flowers and garlands and plastic vines wrapped around trellising. The stage is set up to look as if we are watching Minnie and her interviewer enjoying tea in an English country garden. There's a set of patio chairs. Fancy-lady patio chairs, though – the kind that are made of white metal, with not a sticky plastic lounger in sight. There's an artificial lawn. And, of course, a cardboard Julius.

Minnie is here, overseeing everything, cradling that little dog in her arms, a pink, beaded shawl draped around her hunched shoulders.

There's a ladder and man perched up on the stage scaffolding, screwdriver in his fist, squinting to fix one of the theatre-style spotlights.

When I clear my throat and say hello to Minnie, the handyman looks down at me.

'You'd look a lot prettier if you cracked a smile, love.'

He says this. Out loud! To me!

I don't really know what to say. I'm speechless, and before I can say anything at all, like, 'Um hi, who are you and why are you so concerned about my smile or lack thereof?' Minnie has already jumped straight in there.

'You really ought to mind your manners, young man,' she warns, pointing a brightly painted talon in his direction.

He sniggers. 'Whatever, love. Keep your hair on.'

Minnie laughs. Not like a normal person laugh, but a loud, dramatic, Disney-villain 'HA!' before passing me her dog. 'Take this, my dear girl.'

The prissy ball of fluff and snot scrambles in my arms as I watch Minnie totter towards the ladder.

'Show some respect. No lady likes to be ogled by a piggish lout!'

'Oi! What are you doing?!'

He's perched on a bit of scaffolding. Minnie picks up the ladder in her hands, and moves it well out of his reach.

'That'll teach you.'

The ladder is huge and Minnie looks dwarfed by it. I'm not sure whether it might topple over and squash her but she manages to lay it flat on the ground so that he's stuck up there like a kitten in a tree.

She raises her hand to speak and exposes the baby soft silky palm of her hand. 'There's a difference, my girl, between a bad boy . . . and a bad person.'

Wow.

Minnie.

She totally had my back. She didn't *have* to stick up for me then but she did. What a hero.

'Now, I'm terribly parched. Would you like to join me for

126

a cup of tea?' She juts out her elbow for me to link on to.

The ladder lad makes a sheepish apology from up above and asks me to pass the ladder back to him.

I flash my biggest, cheesiest grin. Like I'm on a Colgate toothpaste advert. Like my dazzlingly white teeth could blind him.

'Is that pretty enough for you?' I smirk. 'C'mon, Minnie, I could murder one of those choc chip flapjacks.'

We walk across the festival grounds, arm in arm, giggling like maybe we're not so different after all.

HoW tHe
oTHeR HaLF LIVE

Today's a shiny, brand new day. Holly and I woke up at the Sea View Lodge with plenty of time to get ready. I had a fresh croissant with one of those mini jars of jam for breakfast, my eyeliner is perfectly symmetrical and the sun is shining. Well, it's kind of shining . . . it's not raining at least . . . for now. Today's off to a good start.

Even Penny seems pretty chill this morning. Her earpiece thing is hanging off her ear but not plugged in. She's telling us all about how the festival began.

She mentioned that she used to work with Tony in the big Bennett's London flagship store 'back in the day', and I cannot bear to look at Holly throughout this convo because I just know that as soon as we make eye contact we will telepathically think, *Ewwwwwwww, do you reckon they were A Thing?!* and then I will imagine

Penny snogging Tony. And then I'll think, *Jeez, imagine Tony snogging* anyone. And now I, Paige Turner, am thinking about snogging Tony. GROTESQUE! THIS IS WHY I MUSTN'T LOOK AT HOLLY.

I take a deep breath and watch that WRONG train of thought choo-choo right out of my mind.

Penny tells us, 'After a difficult break-up I moved out of London to be here, by the sea. I started working in the local bookshop, and fell in love with the place. I just felt like maybe something was missing though. I had got so used to meeting authors and going to book events in the city that it really struck me how little that happens outside of London.'

'I get what you mean,' I nod. 'It's the same in Greysworth – nothing cool like this ever happens there either.'

'Right, you'll know exactly what I'm on about!' Penny laughs. 'I decided that I'd have a go at making it happen here. There are no rules to say that books can only belong to a small number of posh people. Events like this don't *have* to happen in rich, fancy places. People in Skegton like to read – I know that from working as a bookseller here. I invited three authors to speak that first year. We held the talks inside the bookshop. It was a massive hit, with people standing because we ran out of chairs . . .

Since then the festival has grown bigger and bigger. We have a whole team of people organising the scheduling. We ask the people of Skegton who they'd like to invite along. It's my baby. My big, huge baby.'

'I've always wanted to come here,' I gush, since we're having a big girly gush-off, and Penny has turned out to be one of the coolest people ever. (Probably way too cool to have got it on with Tony, but I'll discuss this with Holly later.) 'For years. Ever since I first heard about it. I remember seeing the Skegton Book Festival once on *Blue Peter*. I didn't want to skydive or climb into hidden underground tunnels. I don't even really want to make things out of papier-mâché or raise money for charity, but I did want to come to a festival of *books*. It stuck with me all this time. And now, what I really want is to meet Johnny Hoxton! It's not fair – he's been in the vicinity, treading the same path as me for days now. Holly's spotted him! I can't seem to get near him. I'm starting to think he doesn't really actually exist. I'm probably about as likely to see a unicorn or a reasonably attractive boy native to my hometown.'

'Oh, Johnny Hoxton, yes . . . I think he's mainly been hanging out in the authors' yurt.' Penny puffs out her cheeks, like she must be *exasperated* with people asking after him.

'Oh? That's interesting . . .'

'You didn't hear it from me . . .' She shrugs, pushing her walkie-talkie headphone into her ear and checking her phone.

Penny's said the author tent is off limits, but I'm totally taking what she revealed as, 'Get in there and pretend you work for catering.'

'Right, I'd better be off. Holly, I'll show you where we keep the spare paper bags – it looks like you're running low . . .'

'Sure!' Holly skips after Penny and I grab her arm on her way out.

'Hol, we *have* to get into that author tent,' I hiss, eyes wide.

'Pfffft, sure!' She goes off chuckling, not realising that I'm deadly serious.

This is my chance. I'm finally going to see how the other half live. Well, kind of.

First things first: the plan. Catering staff don't wear the same red T-shirts as we do. They're dressed in black. I need to think fast, so I pick up an abandoned black hoodie from a plastic chair and shove it on. Sorted. Black hoodie, black skirt, black tights. Ninja style.

You've got this, Paige.

Now, I just need to walk in there with the conviction to do so.

I can't do that empty handed.

Think! I stand back and watch the other waitress girls with their shiny hair and cartilage piercings take trays of fresh vol-au-vents and Prosecco back and forth. I just follow in their footsteps and scoop up a tray of some stinky salmon things and dash inside the yurt.

Whoah. I'm in. This place is buzzing wall to wall with people you sort of recognise.

My eyes dart around the room as I hide behind the tray of snacks. It's funny how people just absent-mindedly pick from the silver tray. Nobody says thank you, they barely even look at you or acknowledge you're there at all. It's kind of rude but it's also perfect for spying. No sign of Johnny Hoxton so far.

I move through the crowds, eavesdropping and offering snacks. Then I overhear someone mention Lady Rockwell. My ears prick up. After a few days in her company, I feel like I'm starting to learn an awful lot about her. Maybe I'm even starting to *think* like her – that's the first time I've ever said 'awful lot' to myself. I reckon that if I was on *Mastermind*, I could pick Lady Rockwell as my specialist subject and I'd get so many correct answers that I'd probably win. I listen in.

They're laughing at her. '*I mean, really? Minnie Rockwell?! Oh pur-lease!*' They scoff with laughter and I'm surprised – I feel this rush of . . . what is it? I feel *protective* over Minnie. Like, how dare they say that about her?!

Then I immediately stop myself because I know that Minnie doesn't need me to feel that way on her behalf at all. Minnie Rockwell is definitely a woman who can fight her own battles. I remember her valiantly carrying that massive ladder across the stage. As if she'd be bothered by what some bloke in a corduroy waistcoat has to say about her. LOL.

I deliberately pass him an unwashed glass of wine though. Tiny, secret acts of revenge are best served with a smudge of old burgundy lipstick.

That old couple off the telly who do the book club are here. She's laughing into a glass of wine and he's telling an anecdote to an audience of people, waving his hands around as he does.

I try to squeeze past in my bid to search every corner of the tent, which is a huge mistake because he knocks the tray with his clumsy, storytelling palms and sends the tray of unwanted stinky salmon canapés flying, covering me in bits of fish and parsley.

'Oh dear! I'm so terribly sorry!' he fusses and all eyes are on me, including glances from the waiting staff who surely realise that I'm not supposed to be in here and OH GOD – it is only right now at this very minute that I finally spot Johnny Hoxton across the room!

Like star-crossed lovers, here we are, at last, kind-of sort-of together.

I ignore the telly presenter's bumbling apology and begin to brush the salmony remains out of my hair when all of a sudden –

'THERE SHE IS! THAT'S HER!'

A man in a T-shirt bursts into the tent and points right at me.

I nearly turn around to check if he's talking to me. Kind of like Mr Coates. He was a mad supply teacher. He was never around long enough to know names, so he'd point and say, 'You there!' but you could never really tell if he was making eye contact with you or the kid three seats along.

But nope. This isn't like that at all. The shouty, pointy bloke in the yurt is definitely looking at me.

'THAT'S MY HOODIE! SHE STOLE MY HOODIE!'
Follicles.

I hear somebody else say, 'Isn't she the girl who put dog poo in the crisps?' and before I can even begin to set the record straight, I step right into Penny, who's hands on hips, looking at me like I've got some serious explaining to do.

SPECIAL DELIVERY

Mum would ask me why I'm moping.

I'd insist that I'm not, even though I totally *am* right now.

Mum would actually strangle me, Homer-Simpson style, and ask me WHAT I'm doing fannying around with salmon canapés, flicking them at celebs, when I'm here at the centre of the literary world.

Thing is, I've always been really terrible at being in the wrong. I know I shouldn't have snuck into that yurt, but I had to *try* . . .

I'm sulking because Penny said I have to stay here in the bookshop tent with Tim from now on. Apparently it's too 'risky' for me working elsewhere in the festival. I'm annoyed that I got told, but I'm even more annoyed at myself because it's totally my own fault.

Holly volunteered to work on the door for this American

author who's doing a talk about Getting Ahead in Business. She said she's not into the 'business woman' aspect of Carol Cavendish's spiel (a direct product of Holly picking Government and Politics as one of her AS level subjects and reading the Communist Manifesto) but that she was interested in hearing a woman talk about her experiences of working in a field dominated by men.

I lean on the trestle table, and my self-pity party for one is interrupted as Tim strides over to the desk, golden downy forearms shimmering in the florescent marquee lighting.

'Hulloooo.'

Tim is the kind of man who is incapable of saying hello like a normal person. He'll jolly it up every time, with a wave or a silly voice, and the annoying thing is that I can't resist doing it right back at him, no matter how glum and sorry for myself I feel.

'Heeeeeeeey,' I sing.

He plonks a cardboard box of freshly signed paperbacks on the ground and reaches into the back pocket of his jeans.

'This came for you earlier, when you were with Penny.' He raises his eyebrows from behind the unfashionable frames of his glasses. 'A young man called Robbie asked me to pass it on.'

My heart beats in my throat.

He passes me a small pink and white candy-striped paper bag. Just like the ones they have at his nan's souvenir shop.

'Thank you!'

I am all too supremely grateful to sweet Tim for delivering this to me and also desp for him to bugger off so I can have a bit of privacy.

When I close my hands around the parcel and sit still I think he gets the message. As soon as his back is turned and he's saying, 'Cheerio,' I look inside.

I pull out a red stick of rock with tiny letters spelling out IM SORRY through the middle.

There's a note on the back of a Welcome to Skegton-On-Sea postcard.

Hi Paige,
I feel really bad about what happened with the bike
and the crash last time. I hope I didn't get you in
trouble. Do you wanna hang out? I promise we won't
be involved in any road traffic accidents this time.
Here's my number.
Robbie. X.

GLASS CEILING

The paper bag rustles in my sweaty grip as I gallop like an actual three-legged horse towards the big tent to find Holly.

I'm going to keep this piece of rock forever. Which should be easy enough to do, TBH, since nobody actually enjoys eating rock, do they? I spent far too many excruciating hours in orthodontist chairs to smash up my teeth now.

Those words ring in my ears.

Do you wanna hang out?

I wait outside the Main Stage tent, ear to the canvas as I listen to the audience applause.

I need Holly. I have to get in there to show her the rock from Robbie. The Robbie Rock.

I sneak in from one of the fire exits at the back.

The place is rammed. Spotlights on Carol Cavendish's silky brown bob and red Louboutin heels make it tricky to see who's sitting where in the audience.

The other woman on the stage, dressed in a floral blouse with her blond blow-dry bouncing on her shoulders, speaks into a microphone. '*On behalf of* Voila! *magazine and the Skegton Book Festival, I'd like to thank you once again, Carol Cavendish, and invite members of the audience to ask any questions they might have.*'

I see Holly just milliseconds before the house lights flicker on and I am illuminated, creeping through the aisle hissing 'PSSSSSSSST!' at her.

'Oh, it looks like we have one at the back there.'

I freeze on the spot and slowly turn my head, *Exorcist* style, to see the blond woman on stage pass a microphone through a captive audience towards me.

Oh God.

They opened up the floor to questions.

Nobody ever wants to be the first person to ask a question.

The lights sting my eyes and make me squint.

I guess I'll have to say something now.

Oh God. I haven't heard any of the talk. I didn't even read the blurb of her book while I waited back at the stall.

Oh God. Oh God.

Holly will never let me forget this.

A hand stretches out to pass me the mic. I take it and lick my lips, desperately thinking of *something* to say.

'H-Hi,' I stammer. Feedback from the mic screeches like a toddler in a supermarket and the audience recoil, only confirming that they are all listening and paying attention to what I'm doing. Which is a terrible tragedy. 'Hi, Carol Cavendish.'

'Hi.' Her smile is broad and her teeth are white.

'I have a question,' I lie. 'I was just wondering . . . whether you have tried any Skegton rock . . . during your trip . . . to Skegton.' I wince.

She leans over to her host from *Voila!* magazine and asks what *rock* is.

'Is it some sort of candy?' She frowns and I nod, wishing that I could use this microphone to hammer myself all the way into the earth beneath my feet, like those Whack-A-Mole games they have at the amusement arcade. 'What an unusual question. Well, actually, I'm on a very strict, zero sugar regime . . .' she laughs with her pal on stage, who clearly totally gets the concept of not eating sugar or anything fun, 'so, no . . . I can't say I have tried any of your *rock*.'

'THAT'SGREATTHANKYOU,' I splutter into the microphone before bolting out of the fire escape, fully expecting to find the doctors in white coats waiting for me.

THE BEST THING aBOUT SKEGTON

'I only have an hour for my lunch break,' I explain to Robbie as we walk along the seafront side by side.

'Before you crash any more highbrow literary events?' He smiles as he hobbles on crutches, his right leg held out inches off the ground in one of those hospital boot things. I can't help but feel guilty. I feel like his injury was my fault. Well, Barry the Tiger is also partly to blame.

I walk a bit slower than usual so he can keep up. Robbie is so dreamy, even when he's sneaking out from under his nan's house arrest with a gammy ankle and massive metal crutches.

We stop by a charity-shop window; the shop was closed when I came by this way with Holly. I press my face up to the glass. There's so much packed into the display: a foot spa, a tea set, handbags, a wedding dress and a family of little knitted characters.

'Wanna have a look?' Robbie asks. 'The best thing about Skegton is the charity shops.' He says it so free and easy, totally unaware that I'm having happy heart palpitations over here.

I just love that charity shops have everything. They're time capsules, one-stop shops filled with objects that appear to be totally unrelated to one another. And is there ever anything better than finding something you didn't know you couldn't live without until you see it in a charity shop?!

Well, turns out that there is: it's doing exactly that with a total BABE like Robbie. The only thing I love more than charity shops is boys who love charity shops.

'You can find some proper good stuff sometimes. A lot of the old people of Skegton were mods back in the day. Their old clothes end up in here.' The hangers on the rail squeak as he tells me about a sixties tweed suit he picked up in here for a tenner.

Oh God, the things I'd do – the sentimental items and human organs I'd *donate* to charity – to see him in a 1960s man suit.

We sift through it all. Old jumpers and records and

DVDs. We talk about the films we've seen, the music we hate, the toys we recognise from when we were kids. We giggle and we groan and recoil in horror at some of the weird and wonderful things we come across.

Is this a date? Can a charity shop count as a date? I mean, it's not all candlelit and romantic like it would be in a Minnie Rockwell novel. It smells kind of like stale baby sick, and rather than the sound of violins I hear the old lady behind the counter blowing her nose. But then again, if the Queen of Romance had written my destiny, it would all be very different, I suppose. For a start, this 'heaving bosom' would probs be squeezed into a skimpy corset rather than comfortably plonked into a T-shirt bra I found reduced in Primark.

Speak of the devil.

'Hey, Paige, look!' Robbie points one of his crutches at a Minnie Rockwell book.

'*The Wild Heart of Eloise.*' I put on my best Lady Rockwell impression and he laughs. It feels good to make him laugh.

This is the one Minnie was talking about, that received all of the fan complaints.

I open up the book to the copyright page. It says here that it was published in the seventies. It's got that old dusty smell to it. 'Oh, cool, it's a first edition!' I whisper.

'How do you know if it's a first edition or not?' Robbie asks, leaning his elbow on a clothes rail as he runs his fingers through the floppy bit of his hair.

'Here . . .' I demonstrate, pointing to the page. 'You see this line of numbers?' I'm so, so aware of his body leaning close to me to have a look. He nods, and I continue, trying to keep my cool. 'Well, it's called a number line. And if there's a number one in there at all, it means it's a first edition.'

'Tricks of the trade,' he smirks.

'I wonder why people were so upset about the ending . . .' I think out loud, remembering what Minnie told me about the alternative versions.

'Well, you could just read the last page to find out but . . .' He laughs at me and I nudge his arm. I want to touch him, but I reckon a bantery nudge is just about all I can get away with right now in the middle of the Cats Protection shop.

I test his knowledge of *Now That's What I Call Music* CDs. He's pretty good. I guess we were dancing to the same school disco anthems around the same time, just miles apart. I pay for my old Minnie Rockwell book, hold the door open as he limps out of the shop, and we walk along by the pebbles and the sea.

TaLE AS OLD aS FUDGING TIME

'What's in there?' I ask, nodding towards a grand old building. It looks like it's seen better days. The pink letters spelling out LOCARNO have faded, the way that everything near the seafront seems to.

'Not much, to be honest, unless you're into bingo and OAP tai-chi . . . but it's pretty cool inside.'

I press my face up to the glass, trying to see inside the dark foyer.

Robbie just pushes at the door and it actually opens. Ridiculous.

Now I'm breaking into an ancient dance hall with a total fittie who I barely know. Everything about being here in Skegton feels a million miles from life in Greysworth. Sea and books and boy babes.

I want to know him.

It feels like it would be easy to know him. He's so chill. And delicious. He's the boy equivalent to a bar of Galaxy chocolate.

Shut up, Paige. Stop objectifying this boy by likening him to your fave items from a period-binge Tesco Express haul.

It's quiet and cool inside.

The foyer smells stale, like old cigarette smoke and school canteen chip fat.

There are noticeboards and old photos and that sort of thing. Gold-patterned carpet worn down and threadbare in places. A bit like our old Bennett's shop back home.

'This isn't the cool bit,' Robbie explains. 'It's through here.'

I follow him, past the bar where the shutters are pulled down.

There doesn't seem to be anyone about. It's silent in here, but you can just feel it. It's not like anything I've felt before. It's the history of a place.

We push through a grand set of wooden double doors with music notes painted on them.

'Wow.'

It's huge and it's beautiful. The walls are clad in these ornate oak panels. There are actual chandeliers hanging from the ceiling. And a disco ball. I guess that's a more recent addition. There's a stage, varnished parquet flooring.

Imagine all the people who have danced in this room. Imagine all the stories. My mind races and my heart beats fast.

There's a load of plastic chairs stacked up against a wall alongside a fold-up wheelchair, and a table with a kettle and a radio. They're not as picturesque. They're normal. They must be used for the bingo.

'I know what this needs.' Robbie flicks the radio on and the room is filled with one very loud, obnoxious jingle. *Skegton Golden Oldies FM!*

He twists the dial to find something decent.

A dance track. No, that somehow seems blasphemous in a place like this.

He's watching my face as he flicks through the stations. Then. Yes. This one.

'I love this!' I say it almost before fully thinking about it.

It's an old song. We have it on a Soul compilation CD at home. I see my mum swaying to it immediately, bare feet on the lino kitchen tiles. 'Sea of Love'.

A man's voice fills the room and soaks the oak panels. It's like caramel.

I mime along dramatically. And Robbie does too, leaning on his crutches.

If my life was a film, this would be the shot where I'd spin and spin and on the final rotation I'd be transformed into a total babe in a magnificent ball gown and the Locarno would be magically restored to its former glory. Like some *Beauty and the Beast* trip, Robbie would whirl me around the ballroom, and the kettle and the radio would come to life as humans that somehow still looked a bit like a kettle and a radio.

Fat chance of that happening. He's far too fit to ever be considered a beast and I'm not about to start wearing anything YELLOW. It doesn't suit my pasty complexion at all.

The reality is that I'm swaying and showing off that I know all the words right up until the *I wanna tell ya how much I love ya* line comes up. Then I sort of style it out by looking at my shoes and pretending to have noticed something really cool on the floor. Because what if it looked like I was singing that to HIM. Some lad I just met. He'll think I'm a complete nutter. But then again, the fact I just STOPPED singing along at THAT moment probs just made me look even more freaky. Like not-at-all-casually walking out of the room to get a drink at the precise moment there's a sex scene in a film you're watching with your family.

The instrumental bars that realistically only last a few seconds seem to drag out for hours until the cheesy radio DJ saves my life and the jingle rips us out of Disneyland and drops us back into reality. Back into this abandoned bingo hall.

The next song is another oldie but a goldie. More upbeat. Female singer. Fast. Robbie throws his crutches to the ground, takes my hands and makes me dance. I worry that my palms are sweaty, but thinking *that* makes me sweat more, so I think it's best to trick myself and not think about it at all, right?

It's funny, watching him try to dance with his big hospital boot, hobbling around. We're both falling and laughing. Hysterically.

All of a sudden the door swings open and an old lady in overalls shouts, 'Oi! What do you two think you're doing in here?! Pack it in!'

'C'mon!' Robbie scrambles for his crutches and we bolt out of there, still cackling. I've never outrun anybody in my life before. Sure, the fact he's got a broken ankle has a lot to do with it, but I savour this moment. Eyes closed, rain on my face, feet pounding the promenade, as that total BABE chases after me.

Stitch!

I stop.

We slump into an old brick bus shelter thing.

'Here you go.' He leans over and wraps his very own parka around my shoulders.

Nobody's ever given me their jacket to wear before. Well, excluding my nan letting me borrow a fleece for a walk in the hills. No BOY has ever given me his jacket like this before. It smells so good. Like him. I wonder if my smell will cling to it. I'm kicking myself for the cheese and onion crisps I gobbled up earlier. I can still taste them. As delish as they were, I don't want that to be the lasting impression I leave on this fittie's garments.

We're stood so close to each other. We stop talking. The only sound is rain thudding on the rooftop.

An old man in a mobility scooter reverses into the shelter right next to us. Turns out he knows Robbie's nan. He starts telling us stories about how long he had to wait for a bus last Wednesday. We nod and smile politely.

Robbie raises his eyebrows at me, and I can't help but wonder what would have happened if we hadn't been interrupted by old Frank and his bus pass.

WELL BEHAVED WOMEN
SELDOM MAKE HISTORY

I rush back to the book festival and Holly grabs me immediately. 'Tell me everything! I want to know everything about Robbie!'

I will tell Holly every last detail, even if Nothing Much Really Happened. 'I just have little nuggets of info.'

'Give me all the nuggets!' she demands.

'I promise I will, after Minnie.'

We wheel another stack of Minnie Rockwell books into the marquee that her English country garden stage is set up in. The audience chairs are already filling up with people. There's a happy buzz. Women all around. It's so cool to be in a room full of women. They aren't all old biddies either – all ages, shapes and sizes have been brought together by their love of Minnie.

Holly and I busy ourselves, displaying Minnie's greatest

hits on the sales table. I straighten a pile of *The Wild Heart of Eloise* and I turn to the last page on the sly. Do they or don't they in this one?

The talk is amazing. Minnie wears her most extravagant glittery costume yet and is joined on stage by a journalist who is clearly a huge life-long fan. She knows every one of the Rockwell novels inside out and she talks about the hot men in the books like they're ex-boyfriends that she's still openly into.

We learn that Minnie's a rebel. She's been placing female sexuality at the heart of the narrative for decades. She's sold millions of books, while remaining unmistakably herself. Maintaining this cartoonish, mad version of 'femininity', Minnie has triumphed, just as the women at the heart of her novels always do. She's done it her way and it's working. I'm in awe. And I feel so proud to know her off stage.

She speaks about how many books written at the same time as Minnie's, in the same genre, rarely put women at the centre of the narrative. They even get sidelined in the titles. Other books would be called things like *The Master's Wife* or *The Captain's Wench*, while Rockwell's heroines take centre stage. They have higher ranking positions in society than their love interests. They go out to seek and fulfil their own desires.

'Minnie,' says the fangirling journalist, 'I hope you won't mind me acknowledging that you are still working into your eighth decade. It's amazing. How *do* you do it?'

Minnie laughs and blinks her huge eyes. Because her eyelashes are so big and clumped in mascara, whenever she blinks it looks like she's fluttering her eyelashes.

She talks with her hands, her pink talons in constant motion, and explains. 'As a young woman I used to be shy about birthdays, whereas now I'm rather proud of them, you see. I find they are a real reason to *smile*.'

She winks right at me and strokes the little dog resting on her lap.

Minnie is so cool. I want to tell the world I know her.

WHeN THE LIGHTs GO oYT

It's happening. After days of 'casually' wandering around looking for him, and the shame of the author tent, today's the day we see Johnny Hoxton 'in conversation' at the Skegton Book Festival.

I'm so excited. So-so-so excited that I woke up BEFORE my alarm this morning. That never happens. I can't even drag myself out of bed on Christmas Day until Elliot has prodded me awake with the sharpest-looking presents he can find under the tree.

We file into the Main Stage tent with the rest of the audience.

'OMG, look!' Holly points to the projection of Johnny Hoxton's face, illuminated on the stage behind the leather armchairs and stacks of his book. I'm grinning, clutching my sketchbook to my chest.

It's being recorded for telly. There's a cameraman and

everything. We move past his camera and Holly mouths *'Hi, Mum!'* at the lens.

I plonk onto a seat in the front row and pull her down beside me. We're not supposed to sit in the front row. Well, not really. Seeing as people have paid lots of money for tickets, they're supposed to get first choice of seats. As staff, we're kind of supposed to sneak in and find a spot at the back if there is one. Not for this though. I wanted to make sure that Holly and me see everything about Johnny up close and personal.

My phone buzzes in the pocket of my jeans. It's a reminder I set myself to say the event is taking place this evening. LOL. Like I need to be reminded. Like I'd ever forget.

One of the sound technicians is running cables across the stage.

'Hi, Paige. Could you do me a massive favour?'

I look up into Penny's face, and for a minute I'm convinced that the stars have aligned and she's about to ask me to step into her shoes – to sit in the big leather armchair opposite Johnny and fire away with all the questions on her clipboard and all the questions I have rehearsed in my head time and time again.

'Yes! Of course!'

'Fab.' She touches my arm. 'Okay, I need you to run over to the cafe and grab us a jug of water to have on stage.'

'Oh.' *Is that it?*

'Lifesaver.'

I grumble as I bolt out of my seat, desperate to get this done before I miss anything.

'Oh, and Paige?' I practically knock out two giddy members of the front row as I spin to look back at Penny. 'Two glasses as well, please. Thanks!'

Jeez, Penny, we've already got one Minnie Rockwell on site, we don't need another diva dishing out demands!

I tap on the cafe counter, waiting for what feels like an *eternity* for one of the boys to fill a glass jug with water and ice cubes. I watch the time on my phone anxiously. I can't end up *missing* this talk, not now. I didn't come all the way here from Greysworth to watch some sixth-former with a neck tattoo of a lipstick kissy mark (yes, seriously) ruin a perfectly good jug of water by plonking a load of chopped-up cucumber into it. Gross.

I'm dashing across the festival, past wine-gluggers and signing queues and groups of women with grey bobs and chunky oversized jewellery, winding and weaving until I'm pretty sure I've spilt quite a lot of this water over myself.

I trip into the Main Stage tent, the audience still loud and buzzy with chatter.

Good. It hasn't started yet. I haven't missed anything. Phew!

Penny is being miked up by a sound engineer and she mouths a big *thank you* when she sees me with the jug.

I step up onto the stage and walk across to the little table they have between the chairs. I guess this is where I'm supposed to shove it.

Whoah. The crowd seems huge from up here. There's really, actually, quite a lot of people in this one room. I keep my eyes on the door Johnny Hoxton will be walking through. In my head I keep going over how I'll introduce myself to him. Will I say, *'Hi, I'm Paige, that was a great talk . . .'* or should I maybe go with, *'Hey, I'm Paige. Huge fan of your work . . .'*

FOLLICLES!

I'm lost in fantasy land and somehow knock the jug of water over. It spills over this big tangle of wires leading to a massive extension lead! No-no-no!

The hum of the crowd doesn't suddenly fall silent. The clump of tarantula cables doesn't spark into fireworks or explode.

I squirm. Did anybody actually see it happen?

Be cool, Paige.

I watch the audience.

Nothing.

The sound lady is still fiddling with the microphone attached to Penny.

I sit down at my seat. Even Holly didn't seem to notice.

Yes. Phew. Glad to know I've got away with that. I was beginning to think I'd completely ruined the whole thi—

OH CRAP.

The room plunges into darkness.

IN CONVERSATION WITH

I panic in the blackout. What the *hell* did I just do?

I am going to get in so much trouble for this. Crap-crap-crap-crap!

Seconds stretch out forever in the darkness. I can sense people moving around but the only bits of light come from phone torches so it's still a blur.

I feel Holly move towards the stage and she hisses, 'What do you think happened?!'

It's obviously too dark for her to see the manic panic expression on my face. In the tiniest, wimpiest voice, I confess. 'Holly . . . the lights, all . . . um . . . all of the lights going out . . . it was m-me.'

'HOW?!'

'Shhhh! Shhh! Keep your voice down!' I cannot admit that I BROKE the Skegton Book Festival. Oh God.

My mind races. I see the headlines. I think of how much all of the damage I have caused will cost. I will literally have to work ALL of the overtime hours for ETERNITY at Bennett's Bookshop to pay back my debt. This is it. This is what Tony will walk all the way from Greysworth to personally murder me for. I guess it doesn't matter that I obviously spend an abnormal amount of time thinking my boss wants to exterminate me, seeing as, well, I'll be too DEAD to think about that any more.

The sound lady is looking at the wires and cables by the light of her iPhone and when she moves towards the spillage, I kind of feel like sticking my fingers in the sockets so I can just end it all now.

'Sorry, Johnny, it's a power cut. Hopefully we'll be up and running soon.' Penny's voice. Penny is talking to him! He is here! He is here in the dark. Oh God, LET THERE BE LIGHT! The first real chance I get to see him and I'm too blinded by darkness to SET EYES ON HIM.

The lights flicker on and Holly can't stop laughing. I'm glad she finds it so hilarious. I'm glad one of us does. All I feel is the biggest relief it's possible for a person to feel.

I try to act normal and take a picture of the projection of his face on the wall. *Rock'n'Roll Sketchbook: In Conversation with Johnny Hoxton*. I also twist Holly round in our seats so we can get a selfie with the stage in the background, so it kiiiiiind of nearly counts as a celeb selfie and is tickable on The List.

Johnny slides into the armchair on stage, slouches in his leather jacket and all of that floppy hair. The talk is kind of a blur. It's funny how something you've spent months looking forward to can be over in a flash, quicker than you can say free totebags.

Johnny doesn't say too much, he just runs his fingers through his hair, and stares into the audience with those dark, intense eyes, like a fit Heathcliff. (Well, I say a 'fit Heathcliff' – I know that Charlotte Brontë wrote him as a total fittie, but we watched some dodgy made-for-TV version at school and that Heathcliff was not.) I guess Johnny's been travelling the country on a really intense tour promoting the book (skipping Greysworth of course . . .) but I think he must be really tired. I get properly worn out doing two supermarkets in one day with my mum (she insists on getting specific things in Lidl and picking up other bits from the Co-op. It's long) so I can't imagine how he must feel right now.

But despite that, I kind of wish Johnny would say more about his drawing and writing. They're not talking about the *Rock'n'Roll Sketchbook* as much as I'd have hoped, with Penny instead mainly asking questions about his music career, coaxing him into slagging off his old bandmates. It's kind of massively disappointing. But I realise it doesn't have to be.

What would Minnie do?! She'd take control of her own story.

I promise myself, sat here in this plastic folding chair, that I *will* get to hear what Johnny Hoxton really thinks of drawing. This is what we came here for.

And to do it, I'll show him my sketchbook.

HEARTBREAK HOTEL

I'm beaming.

I realise that I was holding my breath for the entire six and a half minutes that he spent looking through my sketchbook and rubbing the stubble on his jaw. I was hypnotised by all the silver rings on his hands.

It was intense.

'Thanks.' He smiles, passing it back to me. 'And good luck.'

He walks out of the marquee.

Holly tickles my arm.

It's something we always do to each other when we're excited. It's not really tickling. It's not really ticklish. It's just the physical equivalent of going, *Eeeeeee! Oh my God!*

'We did it, Paige!'

It's true. We met Johnny Hoxton! That's why we begged Tony to let us work here.

It's done. He's gone. And he saw my work. I shared my drawings with an actual, living, breathing, famous illustrator. It's something that would have made me want to nervous-vom all over myself a week ago, but spending time with Minnie has taught me to be less fearful about going for that sort of thing y'know. And talking to a practicing artist like him about drawing, and inks and uni courses, makes me feel like it could all be real for me, it could all be within my reach.

'Let's see where he went,' Holly says, pulling on my arm, wiggling her eyebrows. 'Let's stalk him. It's a secret mission. A Day in the Life of Johnny Hoxton.'

'Pretty sure he went into the hotel.'

We follow, keeping a bit of distance so that he doesn't notice us creeping. Then we run along the corridors, our footsteps muffled by the plush carpets. So exciting. I run my fingers along the cream and gold textured wallpaper as we go, then we scram to a stop.

He's ahead, looking at his phone. Dialling. Holding it to his ear.

'I wonder who he's calling . . .' I nudge Holly.

'What's he saying?!' she hisses.

He stops walking. We crouch behind a trolley of toilet rolls and tiny shampoos and cleaning products as we hear him say, 'Hi, yeah, it's me.'

Holly pinches a miniature bottle of shower gel and pops it in her satchel.

'Hol! What are you doing?!' I hiss.

'It's a hotel! They're free!'

'I'm pretty sure that rule only applies if you're actually *staying* in the hotel –'

'Hush, Paige! I can't hear what he's saying!'

HUSH?!

I cover my mouth so I don't let any stray excitement-snorts slip out. My Achilles' heel. It blew my cover in every game of hide and seek throughout my childhood.

My scabby knees crack as we crouch in a clumsy attempt to eavesdrop on his phone convo.

'Eugh. That's the last bloody book talk I do. Forget about the money. It's too tragic.'

He one-handedly rummages through his coat pockets for his key-card thing as he rests his phone between his shoulder and his ear.

'It's all girls in the audience.' He sighs. 'And y'know what? If one more girl asks me to look at her sketchbook . . . Eugh . . .'

Girl. He said 'girl'. But it's the *way* he said 'girl'.

Like having girl fans is the worst possible thing.

Like it's even worse than having fans who are murderers or something.

He said it with disgust.

He has a problem with girls.

Something takes charge of my body and I get up, clumsily push the trolley and knock a few loo rolls tumbling onto the carpet.

'Paige!' Holly calls after me but I'm running – running and hot and full of rage and humiliation.

As I bolt through the corridor, Minnie Rockwell and her entourage bustle out of a door.

'Good evening, Miss Turner,' Reggie says but I can't stop, I can't look at any of them.

Especially Minnie.

If I run maybe no one will see me.

I dash through the big, shiny, rotating door and out into the rain.

To the sea

I don't want to see this any more. Ever. It's all a load of rubbish.

I'm so stupid for making *anyone* look at it.

This way, nobody will have to look at it. Ever again.

The torn pages are there. In the sea. With all the used nappies and crushed beer cans and pollution. And the *Titanic* necklace. And Holly's phone.

'Paige!' Holly shouts at me like I'm a kid playing in the road. 'What the actual *eff* are you doing?!'

'How did you know I was here?' I sob.

I can practically *hear* Holly roll her eyes as she explains. 'I was only, like, five paces behind you the whole time. I know you heard me call your name and I *know* you saw me in the reflection of the New Look window because I waved and you very nearly waved right back!'

She wrestles me and prises the sketchbook out of my frantic, angry hands. I fight her a bit. I scratch her and immediately say sorry.

'Don't be insane.' She's telling me off. 'Your feet are soaking! Come out of the water!'

I look down at the folds of water, lapping over my shoes, moving in between my toes already.

'What are you doing?! This is your coursework – you need this!'

Holly fusses, shaking the water off the torn-up, ripped-out pages of my sketchbook.

'What's the point? You heard what he said, Holly. It's tragic.' *I'm* tragic. The fact I even thought my work was good enough to show him is tragic.

'Well, if you insist on standing in the sea like some sad Antony Gormley sculpture, you could dress appropriately, at least . . .' she says, hopping on one leg as she pulls off her wellies. 'Just put these on.'

'But what about you?' I ask. My voice tiny and silly and babyish as I look at her feet, just socks on the pebbles.

'Bet the wellies don't seem so stupid now . . .' She smiles in an attempt to cheer me up.

'No, Hol, I'm not taking your wellies. If you're barefoot, so am I.' I shiver.

'He's just a prick,' she sighs. 'Just a sexist, ignorant prick.'

I wipe the snot away from my face.

'Shout it to the sea!' Holly screams. 'PRIIIIIICK! Wow! Go on, it really it makes you feel so much better! Do it with me.'

'PRIIIIIIIIIIICK!' we scream into the waves. We do it a few times.

'I BEG YOUR PARDON! WHO *DO* YOU THINK YOU ARE?!'

As if.

Lady Bloody Rockwell, of all people, huddled in a pink shawl, is shuffling along the beach towards us.

SOLID GOLD ADVICE FROM LADY MINNIE ROCKWELL

'Minnie!' I startle. 'What are you doing here?'

'Excuse me? What am *I* doing here?! Me?! When I'm the one not shouting obscenities into the sea, that's for certain. That's no way for a lady to behave. *Beastly girl.*'

I look behind us, towards the promenade, and I see Reggie stood by Minnie's car. She must have told him to take her to us. To me.

'Tell me,' she bellows above the waves and the wind, 'what all the fuss was about back in the hotel?'

'He thinks my work is rubbish. He said it. He said he thinks I'm just another wannabe girl. A loser fan. And that my drawing is tragic.' I crumble, reliving the humiliation in my head.

She blinks at me with those huge, round eyes. She doesn't speak. She understands who I'm talking about.

She just looks at me and I mean really **looks** at me. Her wiry eyelashes bat in slow motion.

I fold my arms across my chest and try to stop the corners of my mouth turning all the way down, the way they do when you feel like bursting into tears in front of a literary legend.

She finally breaks the silence. 'My dear girl. Look at the queues of people lining up to see me, to hear me read a book they've read a handful of times already. They already know the stories by heart. It's been fifty blasted years! They're here for me. For what I do.'

Wow, Minnie. I know and I get it. I didn't really see this moment as an opportunity for you to blow your own trumpet but hey, why not? Be my guest.

'Do you really think they'd be here today if I'd given up the first time a man said my work was no good?'

I swallow and blink.

'*Minnie Rockwell this, Minnie Rockwell that . . .*' She waves her hands around dramatically. 'You know I've heard it all. I had plenty of bad reviews over the years, let me tell you. And men have nearly always dismissed my writing. *Girly books for lonely women.*'

She rests a wrinkly hand on my shoulder and looks me in the eye.

'Of course not everybody's going to like you or what you do. Of course plenty of people will think you're bloody awful! But . . . you're not here to please *them*, are you?'

I look at the grey water, and at Holly, clutching my sketchbook.

Minnie's right. She's one hundred per cent right.

Who cares if Johnny Hoxton doesn't like me? At least I can say *I* like me, and my sketches.

I fall onto Minnie's jewel-encrusted chest and hug her – squeeze her, like she's just saved my life.

'All right, that's enough of that. Now, please, get in the car and sort that face of yours out.'

We bundle into the back of the car. I sit in the middle – Holly holding my left hand, and Minnie to my right. Reggie drives in silence.

I watch the grey sea out of the window.

Johnny Hoxton made me feel stupid for being a girl. If there's one thing I've learnt from Lady Minnie Rockwell this week (well, TBH, there are about one BILLION things I've learnt from Minnie – not least all the saucy things dukes and duchesses get up to in four-poster beds) it's that I should never feel ashamed of being a girl.

Sat here in the back of this car, damp feet slowly

warming up, feeling like I've got two best friends either side of me, I realise it was all worth it. This is exactly how I was supposed to spend the book festival. Actually, no. This is so much MORE than what I signed up for!

YOU RATHER LIKE HIM, DON'T YOU?

'I can't believe it's our last day . . .' I sulk at Holly.

'I know, right?' She sticks her bottom lip out at me, then nods to the pink marble desk on the other side of the tent. 'Can you believe Minnie is doing even more signings?'

'That's what happens after fifty years of bodice ripping, I guess.'

I hold my charity-shop copy of *Eloise*, freshly inscribed by the Queen of Romance herself. From Minnie to me.

Holly opens one of the novels to a random page and begins to read aloud. '*Eloise felt something stir deep within her, an emotion she couldn't ignore any longer!*'

We're falling and laughing at each other when all of a sudden, Holly's face changes. I look back over my shoulder.

Robbie's here. I haven't seen him since our ballroom break-in.

'Hey.'

'Hey.'

'My nan likes these books, right? I thought I'd get one signed for her . . .'

'Oh, yeah, sure. Cool . . .'

A little disappointment goes through me as I put his purchase through. Maybe Robbie's been after Minnie all along. Maybe the scent of lilies and peppermint creams is what gets his heart racing. Y'know, I saw a documentary on Channel 5 a while ago and it was kiiiinda like this. Maybe he's been heart-eyesing her all along.

'Well.'

'Well.'

'Thanks for the book.' He flicks through the pages and shrugs. 'Do you know how this one ends?'

'Haha!' I don't know what to say. This will be one of the last things I probably ever say to Robbie. Talk about pressure. So I shake my head. I SHAKE MY HEAD.

He looks like he might say something, but closes his mouth before he does.

So I fill the gap. 'It was nice to meet you.'

'Yeah.'

Is this it? Is he just leaving on that note? Can I say something to make him stay?

Guess not then.

'Okay. Bye.'

'See ya.'

SEE. YA.

Excellent work there, Paige. See ya, wouldn't wanna be ya! Smell ya later! In a while, crocodile!

What was I thinking?!

I watch him hobble away. He turns a little and smiles at me over his shoulder. And then he's gone.

A liver-spotted, jewel-encrusted hand lands on my shoulder.

Minnie.

'You rather like him, don't you?' she croaks.

I roll my eyes. 'Minnie, we're not all after *all* the lads, y'know . . .' My act doesn't last long. I laugh and grimace. 'Yeah, I suppose I do like him, actually.'

'Well, for God's sake, darling, what are you waiting for?'

I look at her, my mouth agape.

'Do you think I made a life out of women who keep their mouths shut?'

Well-behaved women seldom make history.

'The boy's clearly got excellent taste.'

I'm not sure if she means good taste in girls, or romance novels.

I like him. There, I've said it, I like him. I like him even more than I like getting advance reading copies of books before they're published.

Gasp.

I mean, that's a pretty bold statement. That's a big deal.

So I just think, *Screw it.*

I just think, soon we'll be back in Greysworth and he'll be miles and miles away and I'll be trapped in some hellish French roleplay and I'll be kicking myself for not doing anything about the fact I think he's quite possibly The Fittest Boy I've Ever Shared a Bag of Donuts With.

So I'm pounding the pavements in the rain going after him, and time is of the essence because our train leaves this evening.

I don't really know how long it takes to tell someone you fancy them. I've never done it before.

Well, it's not like I haven't made a move. There was that time I went to the cinema with Patrick Oakley in Year Six. It totally counted as a date as far as Holly was concerned. We went to see some Pixar film on a Sunday afternoon and were the oldest kids in there. No joke, we were surrounded by stressed-out mums and screaming toddlers. I still thought it was dead romantic when he offered me a swig of his Coke though. I felt like there was so much hot chemistry between us that when the anthropomorphic characters kissed on screen, I felt my whole body seize up with tension. Then he leant over towards me. I just went for it, and leant in for a snog, only, horrifically, to find out that he had actually just dropped his retainer on the floor and was reaching to pick it up.

As he rushed to the toilets to rinse the popcorn and hair off of his braces, I sank into my chair and howled with laughter at the singing donkey on screen. We didn't go to the cinema again after that.

I shake that flashback out of my head as I pass the chippie and the *Friends* boxset in the hospice charity-shop window. Go for it, Paige. Think of all the women who come into Bennett's and timidly ask for books like *Feel The Fear And Do It Anyway*.

Yeah. Feel it. Do it.

I'm nearly there at the souvenir shop and I spot Robbie. He's sitting on the bench by the Skegton Tattoo and Piercing Parlour, dodgy ankle stretched out in front of him.

'Paige –'

'So you're thinking of getting a new tattoo?' I ask, pointing towards the templates in the window.

'I would never get a tattoo from there if my life depended on it! My cousin Darren had a tattoo of his daughter, Kayleigh, from here and I kid you not, when he showed me that thing it looked like he had a portrait of Phil Mitchell wrapped up under all the cling film.'

I laugh, feeling the bubbles from this morning's Apple Tango fizz up my nose.

'Robbie, y'know how you read the last page of a book first?'

He laughs, head in his hands like oh here we go again. 'Yes, Paige . . . ?'

'Well, did you ever have those Choose Your Own Adventure books when you were a kid?'

'Oh yeah, I did! The ones where you could pick how you wanted the story to go . . .'

I nod 'Yeah' and sit by his side. We twist so we're face to face.

'So, where does this one go?' he asks me, icy blue eyes turning me to slush.

'Well, I don't know how this story ends but . . .' (I know how I'd like it to end, I think to myself.)

'Choose Your Own Adventure, right?'

That's it. I choose it.

I lean in and make the first move. Put my lips on his.

I feel his hand press on my back and pull me closer to him. This is WAY hotter than anything Minnie's ever written!

Slip him the tongue, Paige! This might be your only chance!

I pull away for air. My lipstick is on his face and, quite honestly, I think *Party Girl Pink* looks even better on him than it did on me.

He laughs, his smiling face centimetres away from mine.

'Paige, I like you. A lot. You came to Skegton and made my whole world feel like a model village. You made it cool to be too big for a place.'

I watch his lips form the words, and make a conscious effort to never, ever forget that he said that.

FEEling MUSHY

'I'm not sure about this, Hol,' I grumble.

'Go on! You'll like it, I promise.' She passes me a little wooden fork as we stand by the cabinet of orange, battered curiosities in the chip shop. One last snack before we board the train back to Greysworth. I'm pretty sure Penny will be glad to see the back of me. We never found out if her and Tony had ever been A Thing, but they've defo got plenty in common when it comes to thinking I'm a bit of a pain in the bum. But hey, one person's pain in the bum is another person's 'sen-SAY-tional' troublemaker, wink-wink. I managed to say a quick goodbye and thank you to Minnie after snogging Robbie's face off. She was surrounded by fans, and *he* promised to sell all the rock in Skegton so that once his ankle heals, he can fix his moped and visit me in Greysworth. Dreamy.

'I promise it tastes better than it looks,' Holly assures me as I hold the polystyrene cup of luminous green snot.

I make sure I have a safe, salty chip lined up to take the taste away straight after.

'Okay, while you nosh it down, I'm going to talk at you.'

'What?'

'While you eat the mushy peas – which isn't even a big deal at *all*, y'know – there's something I have to tell you but I'm only going to tell you once those peas are in your gob!'

'Holly! What is it? What are you talking about?'

'Ah-ah! Eat up, Paigey!'

I groan. Right. Here we go. I stab the wooden fork into the green mixture and scoop some out of the cup. In it goes.

'So, basically, this was left in the Totebag of Doom, and it's addressed to YOU.'

The white envelope is enough to distract me as the salty green mass slides down my throat. It does have my name on it. In fancy, loopy handwriting that I don't recognise.

I tear it open to see pink, perfumed letter paper.

My Dear Paige,

What a pleasure it has been to meet you here by the coast in Skegton-On-Sea!

As you know, I'm currently working on a novel called A Woman on the Edge of Love and I'm writing to ask if you might be interested in providing the cover illustrations. I think you have enormous talent, and I can't think of anybody more capable of bringing this particular story to life than you, my dear girl. That is, if it doesn't interfere with your school and work commitments.

If you are interested, please contact Geraldine, and we can negotiate a fee.

I believe in you, Paige Turner. I just know that you're on the edge of something marvellous.

Your friend,

Lady Minnie Rockwell x

PS – Thank you for introducing me to that dashing gentleman, Tim. He's quite a dish.

I lean back on the chip-shop counter, holding the letter right up to eye level, rereading it to make sure she's saying what I think she's saying. She wants me to illustrate one of her books.

This is mad, mental, amazing. Terrifying.

A book with one of my drawings will be on the shelves in actual bookshops. It'll be in Bennett's.

My eyes sting and I'm pretty sure it's not the fried onions.

Holly gives my shoulders a squeeze, reading it over my shoulder. 'It's *handwritten*,' she whispers. 'Minnie *never* does that . . .'

I place the letter back into the envelope oh so carefully and grin. Minnie Rockwell, you absolute Queen of Babes.

Holly shoves another chip in her mouth. 'We might need an extra ticket for the train back to Greysworth. There's somebody you can't leave behind.'

Robbie? I melt thinking about our kiss by the pier and how perfect it was in that minute. Is that who Holly's on about? About Robbie?

'I've totally nabbed us our very own Julius cardboard cutout.' She beams, smug as a bug in a rug. 'He's coming back to Bennett's in Greysworth.'

'*Sen-SAY-tional!*' I declare, Minnie Rockwell voice. 'Maybe he can seduce the cardboard Mary Berry we have back in the shop.'

Sure, it would be pretty flipping gorgeous to sit opposite Robbie on the train home, but it's cool, I'm not one for skipping straight to the end of a story. And having Holly by my side means we can perfect our vintage Britney singalongs all the way back to Greysworth.

I turn to the girl behind the chip counter. 'Can I have another cup of mushy peas, please?'

Turns out they're actually really nice.

SKETCHBOOK

IF LOST RETURN TO:

Paige TURNeR

THE LIST

- Celeb selfies ☐
  - WIN the jackpot on the 2p Machines ☐
- FIND the best CHIPS in skegton! ☑
  ~~and learn to love~~
  ~~MUSHY PEAS~~ ← RANK.

- SMASH THE PATRIARCHY. ☑

- FIND OUT IF TONY + PENNY
  EVER GOT IT ON 'BACK IN
  THE DAY!
  - DODGEMS | candy floss | donuts ☑

- WIN ~~JOHNNY HOXTON~~ HEART +
  CHARM HIM INTO SHARING THE
  SECRETS OF HIS LIMITLESS DRAWING
  ABILITIES. ☐

THIS IS ALL ONE SWEET, HOT, —THROBBING— LOAD OF RUBBISH.

THIS DOG IS LITERALLY MAKING MY LIFE → HELL

REALLY
THOUGH
Robbie is so gorge that
he makes crutches and
being grounded look
FIT. He's defs the most
beautiful person I've shared
a bag of doNuts
WITH.

A Love Letter To Bookshops

Bookshops are about much more than making money and selling books. They're about the people inside them.

Bookshops are about the children counting pocket money and birthday book tokens while their parents hover, reminding them to say 'please' and 'thank you' at the right time.

They're about rough sleepers, coming into the warmth to sit on a chair and read in peace, in a place where they won't be disturbed or asked to leave for not buying anything.

Bookshops are about debut authors, seeing their own novel on the shelf for the first time, picking it up in their hands, unable to believe that 'it's real!'

They're about grandads describing the layout of the same shop fifty years ago. Bookshops are about finding buried treasure, making unexpected and unlikely friends.

Bookshops are about booksellers giving recommendations for holiday reads and hospital visits, christenings and birthdays and farewells. Break-ups and bereavements and starting school. Student cookbooks and best-man speeches and what to expect when you're expecting. Tracing family trees and building tropical fish tanks and even *knitting with cat hair*.

While I spent a long time thinking bookshops were *The Place* to escape from the outside world, I've come to learn that bookshops can also be very REAL. The connections you make with other book people can be profound. The stories told on the shop floor inside bookshops go way beyond the billions of words printed inside paperbacks on the shelves.

Acknowledgements

Have you seen that clip of Cuba Gooding Jr making his acceptance speech at the Oscars? YouTube it. He's so extra that the music plays him out but he just keeps going on and on thanking everybody and declaring his love for Tom Cruise.

I'm not going to do that. I don't love Tom Cruise. But I do have lots of people to thank for making *Life's a Beach* a real thing.

First big dollop of syrupy gratitude goes to all of the lovely babes at Hot Key. Special thank you to Fliss and Jenny for being such dream editors to work with. I genuinely look forward to your magical margin notes. You turn my bookshop scrap paper notes into actual stories for people to read. Also thank you Alex for designing the cover and making this book stand out as a Serious Fittie.

Once again, thank you to my agent Polly Nolan,

for looking after me and turning me into An Author. I'm so glad to have you on my side. I'm probs a bit smug about it too.

Massive thanks to everybody who has supported *Bookshop Girl* and made it a success. I'm lucky enough to work with some of the best Bookshop Tossers ever at Foyles. You lot are my shoulders to stress-cry on, my staffroom biscuit providers, my hype boys and girls, and most importantly my friends. You've been part of this every step of the way and now you're the people putting my finished books into the hands of teen bookworms just like Paige.

Readers, bloggers, tweeters – thank you for sharing your love for *Bookshop Girl* with me and the wider YA community. Special OMG-Do-You-Know-How-Cool-You-Are thanks to Georgia Nobles (of *Georgia's Bookish Thoughts*) who has given me LIFE with her glowing support for Paige Turner. You're my number-one cheerleader, and my heart melts just thinking about how this goes to show books can bring total strangers together and make us friends.

To my family, my best Cherry-B babes, and my gorgeous Maurice, thank you forever.

I love you all even more than Cuba loves Tom Cruise.

**DON'T MISS THE THIRD
BOOKSHOP GIRL NOVEL –
SET IN PARIS
AND COMING SOON!**

Chloe Coles

Originally from Northampton, Chloe studied illustration at Cambridge School of Art before moving to London. Now in her twenties, she has worked in bookselling since the age of sixteen, squeezing it in around school and university and other jobs. She's previously worked at Waterstones, Blackwells and Heffers and now works as a Children's Specialist and Assistant Buyer at Foyles Charing Cross. All of her hair is her own. People ask her about that. A lot. Chloe sings ('shouts') in a band with her best friend.

Follow Chloe Coles on Twitter @ChloeColes_